— WESLEY ELLIS —

# LONE STAR

## AND THE
## NEVADA MUSTANGS

A JOVE BOOK

LONE STAR AND THE NEVADA MUSTANGS

A Jove Book/published by arrangement with
the author

PRINTING HISTORY
Jove edition/November 1986

ISBN: 0-515-08755-6

Jove Books are published by the Berkley Publishing Group,
200 Madison Avenue, New York, N.Y. 10016. The words
"A JOVE BOOK" and the "J" with sunburst are trademarks
belonging to Jove Publications, Inc.

PRINTED IN THE UNITED STATES OF AMERICA

## The barrel of her gun moved a
## fraction off target . . .

Jessie took a deep breath. "When we reach the first town, you will all be turned over to the sheriff as train robbers."

"I'm sorry," Toro said, "but that will not be the case."

"Give me one good reason why not. I'm the one holding the gun."

"But so is my man standing in the doorway behind you," Toro said, eyes flicking past her.

Jessie did not move a muscle.

"Better believe him, Miss Starbuck," a voice said behind her. "I sure would hate to kill a woman as beautiful as you."

# Chapter 1

Jessica Starbuck could feel the heavy resentment directed toward her. She picked at her dinner and idly listened to Senator Giles Tippet of Colorado introduce her to the huge convention hall filled with cattlemen.

It had been a mistake allowing herself to be talked into being the featured speaker at the Sixth Annual American Cattlemen's Convention in Denver. To begin with, cattle prices were at disastrously low levels and two years of hard winters had decimated the industry. Cattlemen were feeling ornery and betrayed by Washington, D.C., which had done nothing to help them get lower shipping rates to the eastern markets. But even the present desperate condition of the beef industry could not entirely account for the resentment being directed to her on the dais from the huge crowd. No, what they were really angry about was that she was a rich and very successful businesswoman. To most of the old-timers, a woman was good for only three things: making love, making dinner, and making babies.

"Gentlemen," Senator Tippet was saying in a voice that almost pleaded for understanding, "as I stand here and address you today, I know things are very difficult. Our industry is at a crossroads and we must either adapt to the future or face extinction."

"The hell with that bullshit!" a bitter and hard-drinking cattleman from Montana roared. "I say every man in this room would be ten times better off if we got rid of you politicians and opened up the ranges again! Damn the Department of Transportation, the President, and the railroads! Let's go back to the American cattle drives when all it took for a rancher to get his cows to market was guns and guts!"

The conventioneers jumped to their feet and erupted in wild cheers and applause. Senator Tippet, a slight, high-strung man in his fifties, pulled out a handkerchief and mopped his brow. He glanced at Jessie, and she could see that he was near panic.

"Finish the introduction," Jessie whispered, "and let me get this over with."

"I wish to God I'd never gotten you into this," the senator swore. "I'm sorry, Miss Starbuck."

When the cattlemen finally quieted down and poured themselves more drinks they were grinning broadly, for they could easily see how upset Senator Tippet was, and there were few things in life that a rancher enjoyed more than making a politician squirm. One of those things, however, was to teach a rich, uppity woman her proper place. Jessie knew that. Knew that the conventioneers were just sharpening their teeth on the Colorado senator in preparation for ripping her apart.

Senator Tippet must have realized that as well, because his voice assumed a hard edge. "Gentlemen," he said, "and I am beginning to wonder if that is not a misnomer, I ask that you respect the outstanding credentials of our guest speaker and listen very carefully to what Miss Starbuck has to say. You might even learn something of value."

"Like what? How to bake a goddamn apple pie?" a man bellowed.

The crowd roared. They were ready.

"No! Dammit!" the senator shouted. "And if you do not afford her common courtesy, I swear I'll ask her to leave this hall."

The warning was greeted with thundering applause.

2

"To hell with this mob!" the senator cursed. "Miss Starbuck, why don't we leave at once. Nothing can be gained here this evening, and I cherish the memory of your dear father too much to allow you to be humiliated this way."

Jessie's green eyes sparked with fire. Up to now, she had been merely iritated, but that had changed with that apple pie crack and she was mad. "Finish the introduction quickly, Giles. And don't worry about me. It would take more than this crowd of hyenas to run me off the podium. They need to hear what I have to say, and be damned, they're going to hear it!"

The senator nodded. "Some of you know the history of the Starbuck empire," he shouted, beating down the roomful of noisemakers. "But not many. Jessie Starbuck is the daughter of Alex Starbuck of southwest Texas. No man, I repeat, no man has done more for the cattle industry than Alex Starbuck. "You." He pointed to a table of grinning ranchers. "Joel Best, didn't Alex help clean out some of the graft that was going on over near Cheyenne? And didn't he also lobby in Congress to get you and your neighbors a better deal with your cattle rates on the Union Pacific Railroad?"

Joel was a pudgy, red-faced man wearing a big Stetson with a rattlesnake band. Now that he had been singled out, he stopped grinning. "Yeah," he said, barely loud enough for the room to hear. "Alex Starbuck saved my tail, and that of a lot of other men in those parts."

"Then don't you owe his daughter the common courtesy of at least listening to what she has to say to us?" Tippet demanded.

Joel Best flushed with humiliation. He twisted around in his seat and said loudly, "Alex Starbuck was one of the best men I ever knowed. The senator is right. We oughta at least listen to his girl."

"But she ain't nothing but the daughter of a rich man!" a rancher shouted. "Anyone can inherit a finan-

3

cial empire and be successful. Hell, she was born with a golden spoon in her fist. Timber, mining, factories, her old man left her millions of dollars worth of businesses. Why should we, men who have busted out butts to scrape together a ranch, listen to someone who had it handed to her on a silver platter?"

Jessie stiffened. At the far end of the hall, she saw her trusted friend and protector of the Starbuck empire. Ki, half Japanese and half American, had honored this crowd by dressing as conventionally as he could. His long black hair was neatly combed, and he was wearing a suit. Instead of boots, however, he retained his sandals. To anyone else, Ki would have seemed to be an extremely relaxed young man, handsome, with intelligent eyes and slightly Oriental features seemingly in complete repose. But Jessie could almost feel the young martial-arts master's tension. She knew that if anyone in this huge hall picked up something to throw at her or became abusive, he would have to answer to Ki.

"Miss Starbuck has proven herself to be as good a cattleman as her father and every much as good a friend," Senator Tippet shouted. "The fact that she also happens to be a very beautiful young lady should not be held against her!"

A loutish rancher from Oregon named Everett Bonner stood up and glared at Jessie. "When I want to hear a beautiful woman talk, I want it to be in my bed! And if—"

He didn't finish his sentence. Ki was moving off the back wall, gliding through the room, but before he could reach the man, someone else was swinging his fist and driving his knuckles into Bonner's teeth. The rancher went down to stay.

"Dammit!" the young man who had swung yelled. "I want to hear what Miss Starbuck has to tell us! And the next man who insults her is going to get the same medicine as Bonner!"

4

"Who's that?" Jessie whispered to the senator. The young man was glaring at the crowd, challenging them with his eyes and clenched fists. Perhaps thirty, he had sand colored hair, a square jaw, and strong features. Though of little more than average height, there was about him an air of confidence and command.

"That's young Mark Lyon from down in southwest New Mexico. He came in place of his father, who is ill. The Lyon ranch is big, though nothing compared to your outfit."

Jessie stood up and smoothed out the carefully prepared notes she had written for this speech. She would have to remember to thank the man later, though she and Ki could very well handle their own troubles without anyone's well-intentioned assistance. Jessie saw Ki take Bonner's vacated seat so he could be closer in case there were any other ranchers intent on becoming insulting.

Jessie hoped there would be no trouble. Despite the fact that she had worldwide business interests far more profitable than cattle, Jessie loved ranching. Her home and that of Ki was the Circle Star ranch, and she would not have traded it for the most magnificent villa on the Mediterranean or the finest estates and mansions of England or Spain. She was a western woman, one born and bred for the vast and lonesome vistas of the frontier, and nothing pleased her more than a Texas sunrise or watching the glow of sunset fire the snow-mantled Rockies. Jessie Starbuck had charmed and become intimate friends with kings and queens. She had marveled at the intellects of those gifted with genius, felt touched and honored to be the friends of artists, poets, statesmen, and scalawags—but above all, she loved the rugged individualism of the men of the American West. Yes, even when that included men like these.

She took a deep breath and stared out at the sea of weathered, sun-washed, but also very troubled faces.

Jessie momentarily glanced down at her notes. She would not need them; she knew that what she must tell these men had to come from the heart, not from scratched words on paper.

"Gentlemen," she began, her voice strong, but a little throatier than that of most women. "I understand your resentment toward me. There are dozens of men more worthy to address this convention than I. Yes, I did inherit a fortune, but as you well know, fortunes can be won or lost very quickly in our business. I have to say to you that I have increased my father's worth, not diminished it. I've done so because I take pride in the fact that I personally oversee every detail of my ranches. I know when every single calf is born. I have fought wolves and winter, ridden the fence lines during blizzards until I was frostbitten and snowblind."

Jessie took a deep breath. "I ask no man to do what I have not done myself or would do again. I can ride, rope, and brand alongside of any man. I ask no quarter when it comes to the tough, nasty jobs that are a part of everyday ranching. The only thing that separates me from you is the fact that I am a woman, and perhaps I have been given the opportunity to hear and see things that dramatically affect this industry. Things that you all should know. What I have to say is just my own opinion. I expect that you may disagree in part, but please hear me out. Will you do that?"

Her eyes swept over the faces, and Jessie saw that she had softened resistance enough so that they might at least listen.

"To begin with, I have recently returned from Washington, D.C., where I was asked to testify before a congressional committee on the state of western cattle ranching. Gentlemen, let me assure you, I spoke for all of us and I *was* heard. We have been neglected by the eastern politicians and the power brokers. They are all wrapped up in their own quest for industrial superiority with the world. They have a very parochial attitude and seem to believe that we are nothing but a bunch of"— Jessie smiled with a touch of embarrassment—"a bunch of cow-plop stompers."

The cattlemen liked that. They laughed. Not one of them, Jessie would bet, had ever heard it described in quite such genteel terms.

"I assured them that we are also in business and every bit as dedicated to quality and success as the eastern manufacturers. We turn out food for America—isn't that more important than some eastern factory turning out buggy whips?"

"Damn right!" someone yelled.

"Sure it is," Jessie said, warming to her topic. She brushed back her long, copper-blonde hair and lifted her chin with pride. By any standards, she was a beautiful woman, and at times like this she feared her appearance might detract from the message she was so intent on conveying.

"I told Congress that all we asked for was a fair shake. We want reasonable prices for our product and reasonable transportation costs so that we can send beef across this wonderful country and feed people while making a decent profit."

The crowd broke into scattered applause.

"But, with all due respect, we can't go back thirty years and start driving cattle to markets. Barbed wire and towns have killed that day, which I know you regret, but that is the way of progress. We need railroads. We need to start thinking about introducing more of the European cattle bloodlines into our native American longhorns."

This caused a broad murmur of protest. The Texas longhorn was sacred among these men. Ideally suited to the wide-open ranges of the West, the animal could live through freezing winters, blistering periods of protracted drought, and get fat on a rangeland that most of

7

the world's cattle would starve upon.

"I know," she continued, "I love the longhorns myself, but we do need to start thinking about crossbreeding Hereford cattle. Those English beef breeds provide a higher quality of meat, one much superior to the tough longhorn steaks that often chew like saddle leather. Crossbred cattle on our ranches will yield steaks and roasts so delicious and easy to chew that the consumer demand will outstrip any amount of beef that we can produce."

Jessie took a deep breath. "There is one other thing we need to think very hard about, my friends."

She paused dramatically and watched them lean forward in their seats. Jessie had them now. They were poised and ready to listen. "Gentlemen, I submit to you that what we need is to expand our markets."

"To where?" a man called.

"To Mexico," Jessie answered in a firm voice. "Where men, women, and little children are starving."

It was not what they wanted to hear. Their reaction was just as quick and violent as expected, and a loud outpouring of objections resounded in the room. Jessie stood, her hands gripping the podium, and waited. She saw young Mark Lyon and Ki raising their arms for silence and the opportunity for Jessie to finish what she had to say.

Finally, the room quieted enough for Jessie to continue. "I expected your reaction to be negative, but there are a few things you need to understand."

"What we understand," a rancher bellowed, "is that Mexico is about to have another revolution and those people haven't got any money! And what they do have is damn near worthless!"

His comments were echoed by a hundred others, but Jessie's voice cut over them. "And what you don't understand is that we can prevent a revolution by feeding those people in exchange for corn, beans, whatever they

8

have to barter. All right, so they have very little money. But can't you see that if we start helping Mexico by sending them beef, we help ourselves? We are raising too many cattle for the East right now. So, let's create a little shortage and let those people back there know that we would rather help the poor than become poor!"

Jessie tried to drive this wisdom home to these men. "The trouble is, the Central and Union Pacific Railroads, along with the Santa Fe and a few other powerful railroads, control our destiny. We need to make them understand that we have some options. That if they and the eastern politicians don't treat us fairly, we will begin to limit the supply of beef to the East Coast."

"The whole damned country will come down on us, Miss Starbuck!"

"No they won't! Don't you see, we will be viewed as humanitarians by the entire world for helping a starving people. We help a poor, suffering people in addition to our own industry. The press will quickly take up our plight and the politicians will have to fall in line. How can they attack us for saving the lives of the poor?"

"All that sounds just fine, Miss Starbuck," a rancher from Nevada shouted, "but until we get rid of the goddamn mustangs that are stripping our ranges bare, we can't feed anybody—not even ourselves!"

Jessie frowned. Mustangs were no longer a common problem in the West. Most of them had been either shot or captured by cowboys. However, Nevada, with its vast plateau and nearly unmapped thousands of acres of rugged mountains and desert valleys was a final haven for the wild horse.

"Perhaps," a man from another table roared with fiendish delight, "we should all go to Nevada and capture their damn broomtails and herd them down to Mexico. Instead of our cattle, them greaser bastards could eat horsemeat like them sonofabitchin' Apache!"

Many in the room also thought that an excellent suggestion, and gales of laughter filled the huge dining hall. Jessie, Ki, Senator Tippet, and Mark Lyon were not amused.

Mark Lyon shouted. "That isn't the least bit funny! Would any of us have our children eat horsemeat? Do any of you realize that there is a revolution brewing in Mexico and that the revolutionaries have sworn to invade Texas and slaughter whoever they can along our southern borders? That's the kind of men who are stirring the winds of revolution to the south. Maybe, just maybe, if we could help those people like Miss Starbuck has suggested, we could avoid a border war!"

"The hell with that," a Wyoming rancher bellowed in anger. "Me and my friends don't give a damn about the southern border. You live down there, you trade beef for beans. As far as an invasion, we kicked Santa Anna's butt once, we'll do it again!"

The cattlemen from the north stood up and cheered, but those from down in the southwest near the border like Mark Lyon and Jessie were filled with anger. Suddenly, a fight erupted between a tableful of men from southern Arizona and another group from Utah.

Jessie saw a rancher raise a bottle of whiskey and bring it crashing down on another's head. In a moment the entire hall was engulfed in a howling melee of cattlemen hitting, kicking, and gouging. She saw old-timers battling like cougars as tables were thrown over and chairs raised, to be brought crashing down on heads. Some drunken rancher pulled a sixgun out from under his coat and began blowing the chandeliers to smithereens. Uneaten food was being hurled in every direction, and a plate filled with mashed potatoes struck Senator Tippet in the face.

A knot of cattlemen charged the podium and sent it crashing. A drunken cattleman grabbed Jessie and cussed her for being a fool. That's when Ki brought his right foot up in a shap-kick that struck the man's wrist

10

and shattered it. The drunken rancher howled in agony and his friends leaped at Ki, who ducked a blow and delivered a sweep-lotus kick that struck two of the men glancing blows across the jaw and knocked them flying.

But the rest of the men overpowered Ki, and their sheer weight bore him to the ground. Jessie cursed herself for not being armed. She grabbed one man's arm and twisted it behind his back, then shoved him into his friends.

Mark Lyon took on two men and was holding his own until someone brought a heavy silver serving plate down across the back of his head. Jessie tried to get to the young cattleman but there were too many thrashing bodies between them. She saw Ki rear up with a man on his back and another with his arms wrapped around Ki's knees so that those dangerous feet of his were temporarily immobilized. Ki was fighting with the awesome speed and efficiency that made him so dangerous. The man was gentle, intelligent, and every ounce a gentleman until provoked—then he moved with the swift execution of a well-oiled machine. He rarely used more force than was required or deserved and, perfectly schooled in the martial arts, his skills were more than a match against the brawling frontiersmen, whose efforts were usually nothing but a series of windmill-like punches.

But even Ki could not prevail against the overwhelming number of men who were attacking him now. Jessie lunged off the dais to grab a Colt revolver from a cattleman's holster. At the far end of the hall was the mounted head of a trophy longhorn bull, its great rack of daggerlike horns spanning nearly ten feet. Jessie raised the gun and aimed, then fired quickly. Her bullet smashed one beady glass eye. When she had the attention of the brawlers, she snapped off a second shot that blasted out the other eye, just so they would know that she meant to hit what she aimed for.

11

"All right!" she yelled, grabbing the podium and righting it, then banging the barrel of the pistol down hard on the polished wood. "Enough fun for one evening. Next man to raise a fist or a bottle is going to lose it! Now clean yourselves and your tables up and act like grown men!"

The cattlemen unclenched their fists. Plates of food and bottles of whiskey were sheepishly replaced on the tables and about half the room kept glancing at the prize longhorn with two empty holes instead of glass eyes. When Jessie Starbuck spoke again, they listened with great respect.

"I can't make any of you donate a few head of cattle for a drive to Mexico, but I will tell you that, sometimes, we ought to think about those who are really poor—starving poor—instead of ourselves. Look at us! We sit here stuffing our bellies and moaning about beef prices. Hell, half of you over sixty years old are worth a hundred thousand dollars. Is that poor?"

They were studying their plates and fingernails now. They looked ashamed of themselves, and some of them were bloodied and smeared with thrown food. Jessie had trouble suppressing a smile of amusement.

"I've had my say. I'm a woman, but women can understand this crazy business too. Crossbreed your cattle, or in ten years you will find yourself being discriminated against in the marketplace. Your cattle will be worth less than mine, and those who heeded my warning will have no sympathy for you. Think about Mexico and what I said. I have pledged to the President of Mexico that the Circle Star ranch will donate five thousand head of prime beef to the starving people below our southern border. Is that charity? Sure, but also smart business for the good of our industry and our countries. Think about it and let your conscience be your guide. That's all I have to say."

"Now wait a minute," a man offered in a gentle

voice. "We got a little dispute going here at our table."

Jessie relaxed. "What has it to do with me?"

"Willard Morris here says no woman alive could shoot that way again. I bet him a hundred dollars he is wrong."

"Willard, if you lose will you send Mexico a hundred head of longhorn cattle?"

"I will, Miss Starbuck."

Jessie stepped out from behind the podium and fired twice without even appearing to aim. The room gasped in amazement as both tips of the longhorn's spiked horns were blown away.

Jessie tossed the sixgun to the man who owned it. She winked at Mark Lyon and Ki, who were grinning broadly, and then said, "You lose, Willard, but you really don't lose. Those hundred head of cattle will give you a headstart over your heathen friends come the Judgment Day. Might even buy an old skinflint like you a place in heaven!"

She knew Willard well enough to realize that he would take that in the spirit it was intended and laugh along with everyone else in the room.

The roomful of cattlemen rose to their feet and applauded her lustily. Jessie turned away from the podium and returned to her seat at the head table beside the Colorado senator, who was still combing potatoes out of his beard.

"Nice speech," the senator deadpanned.

"Thanks," Jessie said, "I just hope what I said will do our friends here and in Mexico some good."

# Chapter 2

Jessie was encircled by a mob of cattlemen who had cornered her in the hotel lobby. They were all asking her questions about Mexico, those Hereford cattle, and where in blazes she had learned to handle a sixgun so well. Jessie patiently answered their questions, and if someone became belligerent, Ki was standing protectively beside her, ready to gently brush any man aside.

"Miss Starbuck," a heavyset rancher who was obviously feeling his drinks joked, "the thing I want to know is how did a man as ugly as your father have such a good-lookin' daughter!"

Jessie smiled and chose to take that as the compliment it was intended to be. She was used to the attentions of men. They liked to be near Jessie, who was blessed with a face and figure like a love goddess. Her breasts were full, her legs long and shapely. She was narrower in the hips than most women because of the years on horseback. Her eyes changed color depending upon her mood. When happy, they were a soft green, but when angered, they became the color of a storm-tossed sea. Jessie had gone to an eastern finishing school and hated it, but she had learned how to enhance her own natural beauty as well as handle herself with the grace, wit, and charm that was expected of the daughter of Alex Starbuck.

"Miss Starbuck, can we talk privately?" Mark Lyon called.

"The hell with that," several of the men surrounding Jessie grunted.

But she was growing weary of the crush of bodies, the heat, and the smell of liquor and tobacco being exhaled into her face. She had elaborated in great detail about the things she had told them during her speech, and so far, she had at least a dozen ranchers who had pledged cattle for Mexico. Jessie felt pretty good about that. She would, of course, have to hire men to see that those cattle were distributed to the *peones* in real need. Otherwise, they would quickly be confiscated by the wealthy or the strong who cared nothing about the deprivation of their fellow Mexicans. She would send a telegram to the Circle Star ranch and inform her men to move the cattle south at once.

"Give the lady some room!" Mark Lyon shouted as he gave up being patient and began to bull his way through the throng of packed bodies toward Jessie and Ki.

"It's an honor to meet after hearing about you and your father all these years," Mark Lyon said, reaching out and taking her hand. "I've also heard of you, Ki."

When the two men appraised each other, Jessie noted that they were about the same build, one dark, the other fair, but each very handsome.

Ki nodded with a half smile. "Not all bad, I take it?"

"All good, Ki. I was told that you are like a brother to Miss Starbuck. Is that true?"

"Yes," Ki said. "I am her loyal friend."

Mark was reading Ki's expression carefully. It seemed quite obvious to Jessie that the New Mexico cattleman was making sure exactly what the relationship between her and Ki really was. He was also quite pleased at the word "friend" that Ki used, because it said a great deal. Ki was an extremely attractive man to the opposite sex, but their relationship was purely as friends, nothing more, but nothing less. Jessie loved Ki

15

deeply and that love was reciprocated. More than once, they had risked their lives for each other, and yet they seldom touched, each almost afraid that some delicate balance might be tipped and be irrevocably flawed.

Mark Lyon looked into Jessie's green eyes. His own were soft blue, a trifle yearning. "It's vitally important that I talk to you alone," he said.

"I'm sorry. I deeply appreciate your taking my part a while ago and trying to protect me, but you will have to accept my simple thank you and leave it at that. Ki and I are ready to retire for the evening. We are leaving tomorrow morning for Seattle."

"But you can't, Miss Starbuck!" Mark said with genuine alarm.

There was something so desperate about the way he said those words that it made Jessie blink, as much out of curiosity as surprise. "And why not?"

"Because I have something to tell you that will change your plans. Something that could change the course of history."

Jessie doubted his words. Many men had tried to use exaggeration, flattery, or even deception just to gain a few extra moments with her. She had no doubt that Mark Lyon was one of those men.

"You don't believe me, do you?"

Jessie took the young cattleman's arm. He was very earnest and she did need an excuse to leave this clot of men. "All right," she told him. "We shall have a few moments alone together."

The cattlemen groaned, but they had learned better than to try and force their wishes on Jessica Starbuck. They grudgingly gave way and let Jessie, Mark, and Ki pass out of the room.

"I will be upstairs," Ki said. The implication was very clear. Ki would never interfere with Jessie's involvement with other men, but he was always ready to help her if she faced trouble.

16

The stairway was blocked by conventioneers and Jessie did not relish the idea of making her way through them. "Why don't we go for some fresh air and a short walk," she said.

"I'd like that very much."

Outside, the evening air was cool after a very hot summer afternoon. There had been showers, but they were almost bathtub warm, and when they hit the hot street surface of downtown Denver, the rain steamed. Now, however, the stars were twinkling and the moon was a wedge of beaten gold. Carriages and buggies crowded the streets and the tinkle of piano music floated on the air.

"I like Denver," Jessie said, admiring the broad street and the dark, silhouetted Rockies hovering to the west. "It has so much vitality. It reminds me a little of Seattle."

"Seattle? I've never been there. What, may I ask, is taking you there?"

"I have some logging tracts that we need to reseed, and there are a few problems with our lumber mills."

"I see." He fell silent as they strolled along together.

Jessie glanced at him. In the soft lamplight, she sensed that he was being pulled by some inner struggle. "You made a very interesting statement to me inside the hotel. Something about changing the course of history. I hope you are not planning to simply clam up now that we can speak privately."

His head lifted and he sighed. "No, I won't clam up, Miss Starbuck. But I swear I did not exaggerate the importance of what I had to say. Have you heard of my father?"

"I know he was a general in the Confederacy. A natural-born leader respected by both sides of the battle-field."

"Yes. My father is quite a man. Not nearly as financially successful as yours, of course, but very much

17

loved in our part of the country. Did you know that he was, until last year, the representative of President Rutherford B. Hayes to the government of Mexico?"

"No."

"Well, he was. He only resigned that post to devote all his energy to Mother, who was very ill at the time and desired to come home from Mexico City. Six months ago, my mother died."

"I'm sorry." Jessie meant it. She could tell from Mark's tone of voice that the loss had hurt him very deeply.

"You would have liked her, Miss Starbuck. She had your fire and beauty. My mother was never one to duck an issue, and I guess that is why I so admired your speech this evening."

"Mark, would you please call me Jessie?"

"All right." He took a deep breath. They had reached a downtown park, and Mark took a seat on a city bench. "When my mother died, my father soon returned to Mexico. He needed to get away for a while, and I thought it would be good for him. What no one north of the border realized, however, was that a revolution was stirring. The newly elected President Manuel González is also is also a good friend of my father. Like yourself, we are convinced that González means to bring about major social reforms that will benefit all the people and not just the rich. But he needs time. When I heard you say the same things tonight, I knew that we had to work together."

"Now wait a minute," Jessie cautioned. "I'm doing all that I can to send beef to Mexico."

"I know that, but there is something else that is needed even more than beef."

"What?"

"Horses," Mark said. "González's army has been decimated by thievery and corruption among his generals. He has finally weeded out the unjust and unwor-

18

thy, but not before one thousand of his horses were illegally sold or stolen from the Mexican army. He must have horses to have any chance of protecting the border people and of resisting the revolutionary movement."

Jessie nodded. She had not realized that things were so desperate with González's new government. "I can send horses along with the cattle."

Mark's eyebrows raised. "Jessie, President González needs at least a thousand good horses. The previous government left no money to buy them. Always in the past, the new government would simply take whatever it needed to supply its army. González knows that to do this would be to rob the poorest and create a breach of faith among his people."

"So he is caught. He can't afford to buy horses and he can't afford to appropriate them for the army he needs to quell a bloody and unnecessary revolution."

"Exactly," Mark said. "President González wrote this letter to my father begging for his help."

Jessie watched him remove the letter from the inner pocket of his jacket. "May I read it, please?"

"It's in Spanish."

"Of course it is. I have found it necessary in my business dealings to be fluent in many languages."

She took the letter and read it quickly. The message was brief, a little desperate in tone, and quite specific. President González did need a thousand sound riding horses and had no money to pay for them. What little money he had to rebuild his government was being spent on food and clothing for his small army. González also mentioned that the new revolutionists, under a man named Armando Escobar, were stirring up the people to form armies and reclaim the land they had given up north of the Rio Grande. This was, he noted, suicidal, but the *peones* had always followed false prophets and dictators who made wild promises. Had not they risen up and followed the despot Santa Anna north to slaugh-

19

ter those at the Alamo? Could not something be done?

Jessie folded the letter back up, slipped it into its envelope, and handed it to Mark. "Why doesn't the United States government simply give this man the necessary funds or supply him with the horses?"

"Because that would make it seem as if this country was supporting González! The Mexican people are very sensitive about foreign intervention into their affairs. The wounds from the Mexican War in which we invaded Mexico City and defeated their country are still raw. To admit that we helped González would be like giving him and his government the kiss of death."

That made sense to Jessie, and explained why this matter was of a delicate and highly secretive nature. "Then we must find a way to help that man," she said.

"I think I already have. You see, the reason I was sent here instead of my father was that he has never really recovered from Mother's death. He hasn't the strength to push the men at this convention into donating horses for a cause they do not care about or fully understand."

"And that's why you came?"

"Primarily. But then when I saw how rudely they treated your suggestion of donating an overabundance of beef to Mexico, I knew that I had no chance at all of getting good saddle horses. Cattle prices may be off, but the value of sound riding horses is still very high."

"That's true enough. In fact, we have taken to breeding our own replacement cowhorses."

"I'd like to talk about that someday," Mark said, "but right now, what I have to say might sound crazy, but it could work."

"My father and Ki have taught me enough wisdom to know how to listen before closing my mind to any new idea. Go ahead and tell me what you have in mind."

He pushed his Stetson back to reveal a broad forehead that gave an indication of high intelligence. Mark

Lyon looked down at her and said, "The fellow from Nevada gave me the idea that we could maybe help the Nevada ranchers, and also help Mexico at the same time by capturing mustangs."

"Oh, now wait a minute!" Jessie said, shaking her head. "President González needs saddle horses, not unbroken mustangs."

"He has plenty of men to break them properly."

"It could take years to catch a thousand head of good horses."

"We don't have that long," he answered. "We'd have to do it by November first in order to get them ready to ship before winter."

"By ship, you mean out of, say, Elko, Nevada?"

"Yes. From Elko over the Rockies to here, then switch railroads and send them down to my country around Deming, New Mexico."

Jessie snapped her fingers. He had made everything sound so very simple. "Just like that?"

He grinned. "Nope. It will be a dogfight every mile of the way. And I had better tell you something else, Jessie. Once the Mexican revolutionaries discover what we are up to, they'll come gunning. They won't quit fighting until we either deliver those mustangs, or die trying."

"I'm in the habit of finishing what I begin," Jessie said.

"I never doubted that. But I want you and Ki to know that it will be dangerous."

Jessie thought it over carefully. Her business in Seattle could wait, and she employed the best and brightest men possible just so that she and Ki had the freedom to take on unexpected problems such as this. "If Ki and I were to help you, how can you be so sure that these revolutionaries under Armando Escobar will know what we are up to?"

"I can't be," he replied. "I just thought it would be

21

fairest to admit they might be shadowing me right now. They knew that the only man President González could turn to is my father. I assume they sent spies to watch him and that they followed me here."

"Then your life may well be in jeopardy."

"And so would Ki's and yours be if you both go with me."

"I have never been mustanging. Down in our part of Texas, the mustangs were caught by the Comanche and Kiowa years ago. Might be fun."

He shook his head. "It won't be, Jessie. It will be hard and dangerous work. We don't have much time. I have some money to hire men, but I'd rather wait and hire them when we reach Nevada. Less chance of attracting attention."

"Good idea. But when we load those horses at Elko, the secret will be out. The news will flash across the telegraph lines. When we reach Denver, there will be dozens of reporters. You can't hide a thousand head of wild mustangs, and the news will raise a thousand questions."

"We can face that when it comes," Mark said. "The future of Mexico and maybe a lot of people along the border depends on our success—or our failure."

"Your idea is pretty farfetched. I really doubt if it has any chance of working. From what I know of mustanging, they are very difficult to catch."

"There are mustangers who can be hired to teach us," Mark said.

Jessie looked him right in the eyes. "If I ask Ki and we decide the idea will fail and we are not interested, what will you do then?"

"I'll be brokenhearted, of course. Not having someone as beautiful as you to keep me company will be a severe loss." His grin faded. "But I'll go to Nevada alone if necessary. Spend what money I have and do the best I can."

"That's what I thought," Jessie said, rising to face him. "I like your spirit too, Mark. Come on then, let's go discuss this with Ki."

"Do you discuss everything you do with him?"

Jessie suppressed a smile. "Not everything. Just what is dangerous."

He brightened. "Sounds only fair."

Ki listened very carefully, and when Mark Lyon was finished, he said, "The Seattle problem can wait, Jessie. This sounds like the most important thing that we could be doing right now."

"I agree." Jessie pursed her lips. "Then we shall leave for Elko, Nevada, tomorrow. In the morning, I'll send telegrams to Seattle as well as the Circle Star saying we will be delayed for a while."

"Quite a while," Mark said.

Jessie shrugged. "I intend to help financially, of course. I will see that every qualified mustanger in that part of the state helps us. I'll pay top wages and expect fast results. If it is true that President González needs those horses so badly, then we must not delay."

Ki listened for a few more minutes before he said, "What about these revolutionaries you believe might be following you, Mark? Will you recognize them?"

"No, and they may not be Mexicans, either. To be honest, they may not give us any trouble at all."

"They will if they know your intentions," Ki said. "We must be on guard for any kind of treachery."

"Agreed, but I don't think that is something we have to worry about until later."

Ki smiled. "It is often at times when we least expect it that trouble comes." The martial-arts master glanced at the door and lifted his finger to seal his lips.

Ki moved stealthily to the closed door. His ear pressed to the wood and he listened for a moment. Then his hand closed over the knob and he yanked the door open.

The man who had been standing in the hallway eavesdropping was caught totally by surprise. He was Mexican, a smallish fellow in his thirties with shaggy hair and a half-dozen clean bath towels draped over his arm.

Ki grabbed him and, with a twist of his body, threw the man inside to crash against the opposite wall.

The intruder began to babble in a mixture of Spanish and English. As near as Jessie could tell, he was trying to explain that he had merely been listening to see if he could enter the room and replenish it with fresh bath towels.

He was lying. Jessie knew that, though it would be impossible to prove. "The towels were changed this morning, Señor. You are not telling us the truth. Why were you listening at our door?"

"Oh, Señorita, I do not lie! I swear it! Please let me go!"

But Ki had other thoughts. He also knew that this man had been spying. It was important to find out who had sent him. "Get up," Ki ordered, moving toward the man and standing before him with folded arms.

The Mexican rose to his feet. Erect, he seemed larger than he had previously appeared. There was an ugly scar along one cheek. His eyes lost their subservient look and grew hard. "Let me go," he said in almost perfect English."

"First the truth," Ki said. "Who sent you to listen to us?"

The Mexican dropped his towels to reveal a wicked knife. "Stand back or I kill you," he warned.

Mark reached for his gun.

"No," Ki said, "I want this man alive."

"But—" One look at Ki and Mark forgot his protest.

The Mexican could not believe he was hearing correctly. Not five feet before him stood the Oriental and the man was not even armed. "I am leaving now," he said. "Do not try to stop me."

"Take one step forward and you will be in pain," Ki said.

The Mexican blinked. His knife began to slice the air between them. Suddenly, he lunged, knife held low and cutting edge up. No one had to tell Jessie that the man was a veteran knife fighter who knew how to handle cold steel.

The blade cut a swift arc toward Ki's belly and Ki seemed to move faster than the eye could detect. One instant the knife was driving for a killing thrust, the next it was spinning away and Ki's hand had swept up in a *migi-shote* blow that brought the hard edge of his hand slashing into the Mexican's wrist, breaking it as if he had been struck by a tree limb.

The Mexican staggered. Ki stepped back. "Now you will tell us who sent you."

"No!" Then, before any of them knew what was happening, the man spun around and dove through Jessie's third-floor window.

They heard a heavy splintering of wood and then a scream. Jessie reached the window and peered down at the lower awning, which the Mexican had no doubt expected to break his fall. The awning had been weak and his falling body had torn through it on his way down. From the angle of the man's head as he lay faceup in the street below, it was clear that the Mexican had snapped his neck.

Ki was disgusted with himself for allowing the man to be killed. "I'll go down and search his pockets, but I don't think I will find anything of interest."

When he had left, Jessie poured two glasses of brandy. She was not unaccustomed to sudden death, yet she had never really gotten used to it. Handing Mark Lyon a glass, she said, "It would seem that we have no time at all to lose in catching our mustangs."

"I'm sorry. I thought we might avoid trouble, at least

25

until we had finished the roundup. Are you sure that you and Ki want a piece of this?"

Jessie smiled a little sadly. "We've already bought into this game, Mark. And it is one we must win."

She raised her glass in a solemn toast. "To no more killing and to mustangs for Mexico."

He nodded. His face was grim but set with determination. "And to you, Miss Jessica Starbuck, the most beautiful woman in the West."

★

# Chapter 3

They had taken the train north to Cheyenne, where they connected with the Union Pacific line. Their train had carried them across the great plateau of Wyoming, then labored over the Wasatch Mountains and dropped down into Salt Lake City. From there they had crossed the huge Salt Lake basin and entered the high desert-sage country that flowed west into Nevada. Jessie had crossed the country many times by rail, but never ceased to be amazed at how great a challenge it must have been to build this mighty railroad that spanned the western two-thirds of the American continent.

Jessie had been a very young girl, but she still remembered the tremendous celebration that had swept across America with the completion of the transcontinental railroad in 1869. It had been considered an impossible feat at the time, especially for the Central Pacific Railroad driving out of Sacramento and needing to conquer the towering Sierra Nevada Range. Had it not been for the Chinese coolies and the rugged Irish who had come to give their lives and labor, the railroad might never have been completed. At Promontory Point, where the two great railroads met, Jessie saw a small rock monument commemorating one of the greatest engineering feats in history.

As they approached Elko, Jessie could see the effects of drought. The grass should have been green, the cattle fat, but neither was the case. "This looks a lot like the

27

country I come from," Mark said. "What does your part of Texas look like, Jessie?"

"It's as dry as this and has high chaparral. We wear heavy chaps to keep thorns from raking our legs and the sides of our horses. Longhorn bulls the Mexicans call *cimarrónes* hide in the thickets, which cover hundreds of acres. It is very dangerous to go after a *cimarrón* because the thickets close over you to form tunnels. Roping in a brush tunnel is an experience even the finest *vaqueros* do not enjoy."

"You said at the convention that you can rope."

"Yes, but I am no expert."

"Ki, what about you?"

"I am even less of an expert than Jessie," he said.

Mark Lyon chuckled. "Well, that makes three of us, because I never claimed to be the best roper either. I think one of the first things we need to do is to hire a top mustanger and a good crew of men who know this country and mustanging."

"Sounds reasonable," Jessie said. "I've found the best way is to put out posters or an ad in the paper, if there is one in a town this size. You get a better quality of men than if you just start hitting all the saloons."

"Then that's what we'll do. Only remember, we haven't a lot of time."

Jessie looked at him closely. "You keep telling me that. Is there something else I should know?"

"Like what?"

"Like exactly how much time do we have? I'm beginning to think that perhaps President González is in a greater danger than you have told me."

Mark lighted a cigar and blew a stream of blue smoke up at the roof of the dining car. "My father's friends say that González needed these horses months ago."

Jessie frowned. "Has it occurred to you that we might find all of this is in vain? That if and when we do get the mustangs to the border, we'll find the revolution is underway and another government in power?"

"I've thought of that."

"Then what would we do?"

"Sell the horses to the United States Army, because they'll need them when Mexico invades Texas."

"We split the profits down the middle."

"Agreed." Mark smiled. "Unless the Starbuck empire chooses to donate them to my Rocking L ranch."

"No," Jessie said. "The reason I am a successful businesswoman is that I do not make gifts to people who don't need them."

"What makes you think I don't?"

"You just don't strike me as the kind of man who requires charity—or even one that would take it if offered."

He laughed. "You're right, Jessie. Here comes Elko. It'll be good to get off this train and back into the saddle again."

The train began to slow and big clouds of steam rose up from under the wheels of the locomotive. Up ahead, a boom was being lowered from the huge water tower. When all the passengers disembarked at the railroad station, there was a flurry of activity. Cowboys greeting other cowboys, ranchers and their families being reunited and, on down the line, pens of horses and cattle being readied for loading.

"Look at those horses," Ki said, pointing down the tracks. "I'll bet they are mustangs."

Jessie nodded. She had seen just enough mustangs to recognize them as being horses generally a little smaller than normal. Tough and wiry, they always had a wild, unkempt look about them until broken to ride. But when grained, brushed, and shod, they blossomed into very nice horses.

"Let's see if those men are interested in a job," Mark said, not waiting for an answer, but heading down the tracks with Jessie and Mark beside him.

There were about eighty head of horses and they were in a big railroad stock pen. Up close, Jessie could see how really pathetic the animals were. They could not have averaged seven hundred pounds each and their ribs and backbones poked sharply at their hides. One especially sorry creature had bloodstains all down the insides of his legs. Jessie realized this had been the stallion and that he had been range-gelded and driven to this railhead before his wound had properly healed.

"I'm not sure these are the kind of men I want to hire," she said, watching the mustangers as they worked the defeated animals toward the loading chute. Jessie could not help but feel pity for these poor animals. Once proud, now their heads hung low and their eyes were dulled with misery.

"Maybe it's not their fault," Mark said. "If the range is in as bad a condition as those ranchers from Nevada said it was, then it might be a mercy to capture them before they starved."

Mark was right, but Jessie hoped that the mustangs they hunted would not all turn out to be in such terrible condition.

"Who is the boss here?" Jessie asked an old cowboy who wore a sweeping gray mustache and a slouch hat that had long since forfeited both color and shape. He was thin and bent, way past the time when he should have traded a horse for a rocking chair. Despite that fact, he had a pleasant face and was whistling a happy tune.

He reined his horse in and took a good look at her, squinting with appreciation. "Ma'am," he drawled, spitting tobacco juice at the mustangs, "whoever you want to be. But my name is Pete."

"Did you catch these mustangs?"

"Nope. Fellas that did ain't here right now. Me, I just haze these sorry critters for the railroad. I'm way too

30

damn old and stiff for mustanging anymore. But I used to be one of the best in Nevada. I caught mustangs before they was worth anything 'cept to be made into cowhorses. Didn't pay worth a damn then; still don't. Nuthln' more fun, though, 'cept . . . well, never mind that. I sometimes talk too much, ma'am."

Jessie recognized an old-timer who had a lifetime of stories to tell and no one very interested in hearing them. "Pete, what is the man's name that caught these and where might he be found?"

"Name is Hob Ellis and he'll be bringing in a bunch more this afternoon. Fact is, he better be before the next train movin' east comes through. He's got a contract for another eighty head for the slaughterhouse in Chicago."

"Where are these going?"

"Slaughterhouse in San Francisco, ma'am."

Jessie had been afraid that was their destination. "These would be pretty decent mounts if they were cared for, fattened up, and properly trained."

"No feed for horses in this country," the old mustanger drawled. "Any feed you can buy hereabouts will be for cattle and it'd cost you plenty."

Mark said, "Do you know how much these horses are bringing in San Francisco?"

"Ten dollars. Doesn't matter if we send 'em five or five hundred. Ten dollars a head is what they'll bring. Slaughterhouses will take all we can send."

Jessie curbed her annoyance. "Pete, we were told this country was being overrun with mustangs."

"Not around these parts, ma'am. They all been catched or shot this past year when the grass started withering and the water holes drying up."

Jessie cussed silently. If the conventioneers from Nevada had been lying, then they'd wasted precious time by coming here.

"Where *can* we catch mustangs?" Mark asked bluntly.

"What you want to do that for? Ain't much money in it. Dangerous as hell. You folks ain't dressed like you need to kill yourselves for the likes of these ten-dollar bagsa bones."

"We'll take this bunch at eleven dollars a head," Jessie said.

"These?"

"Yes. Is there a problem?"

"Ma'am," Pete said slowly. "I got orders to load these horses into that boxcar. Now, if that train pulls out and you should change your mind and not want the horses, Hob Ellis would just naturally stomp my head in."

"I understand." Jessie reached into her denims and pulled out a leather wallet, one made especially for her by one of the Circle Star's cowboys. It was beautifully stitched and had her initials carved into the leather along with the Circle Star brand. She selected a hundred-dollar bill and handed it to Pete. "This ought to solve that problem."

Pete grinned wide. Three of his front teeth were missing. "Yes, ma'am! Say, that wallet of yours, Circle Star. Ain't that down in Texas? I cowboyed there some years ago. Comanche were still raiding then and the Texas Rangers had all the trouble they could handle. I saw Sam Houston in Austin, bigger'n life he was. Circle Star, can't quite recollect who owned it, but it'll come to me." Pete shook his head. "Damned memory is going to hell. Forgettin' names is the first of the four well-known signs of senility."

"Pete—"

"Aren't you even going to ask me what the other three signs are?" he asked with a devilish wink.

Jessie nodded. She would hear them anyway.

"First you forget names, second you forget faces. Third you forget to button your pants after you take a leak . . . and fourth, hang on, it'll come to me . . . oh,

32

yeah, fourth you forget to unbutton 'em when you take a leak!"

Pete laughed uproariously, and even Ki joined in.

Jessie waited until Pete stopped laughing. She did not want the news to be out that Miss Starbuck was buying mustangs. It could cause all sorts of problems, including very much unwanted publicity by the local paper. The Starbuck empire was so far-flung and powerful that it always set people into trying to figure out how to skin her and her enterprises. Men usually assumed a pretty woman meant an empty head. Jessie did not especially enjoy having to repeatedly prove them wrong.

"Here's another twenty dollars for you to keep that bit of information to yourself, Pete. Also, I'd like to know where we can find mustangs."

The smile died on the old-timer's creased and deeply tanned face. He pulled at his tobacco-stained mustache and grimaced. "I can tell you where you can chase thousands of then, but you won't want to hear me say it."

"Try us," Mark said, leaning forward with anticipation.

"Southwest of here about eighty or a hundred miles. Best mustang country in the world."

"That kind of distance isn't going to stop us."

"Nope, I reckon not, but Chief Three Kills and his raidin', scalpin' bunch of Paiutes just might."

Mark swallowed noisily. "Chief Three Kills? I never heard of him."

"Not many have. He was raised by missionaries and is as educated as any of us. He got beat up too much in the city and wound up killing a man. Before they could lynch him, he ran away and grew up in the wildest country down south you ever seen. Started attracting misfits and reservation jumpers like himself. Now he rules the central part of Nevada. You leave him alone,

33

he leaves you alone. But you try and take his wild horses or his pine nuts or deer, he'll take your hides and stretch them over a juniper tree."

Jessie frowned. There were still places where the Indian held control. The Apache remained unconquered in the most desolate parts of the Southwest, where water was scarce and the land unfit for ranches or farms. Central Nevada was brutal too, a million acres of sun and wind-blasted mountain ranges and damn little water. It was a land where only the Indians, mustangs, rattlesnakes, and scorpions thrived.

"If we could talk to this Chief Three Kills, do you think he might let us buy mustangs that we catch?"

"Dunno," Pete said, shrugging his thin shoulders. "What he might do is let you catch the mustangs, then kill you and keep your money."

"I take that to mean he is not a man of his word."

Pete looked her dead in the eye. "Why should he be, we never kept ours."

Ki smiled, because that was the God's honest truth.

"Ma'am, let me tell you something. Hob Ellis and his boys are tough, real tough. But they ain't stupid and they won't go down to play in Chief Three Kills' backyard for no amount of money. You can talk to him, but you'd be wasting your breath."

"Where is Hob Ellis catching these mustangs?"

"That's supposed to be a secret."

Jessie handed him another twenty dollars.

"But it's not a very well-kept secret," Pete decided on second thought, "so I guess it wouldn't hurt to tell you, if you didn't tell anyone else."

"We won't."

"Promise?"

"Yes, dammit!" Mark said impatiently. "Now, where do these horses come from?"

"About fifty miles south of here, along the southern end of the Ruby Mountains. It's about the only place

34

where there is still good grass and water. There are a few ranchers down that way and they shoot these horses on sight. I suspect they also pay Hob four bits for each one he captures."

"Then that's where we'll go."

Pete scratched his jaw. "I was you, I wouldn't," he said quietly.

"Why not?" Mark asked with exasperation.

"I can guess the answer to that," Ki said. "The reason is that Ellis considers that his personal mustanging ground and doesn't want any competition."

"Say, you're pretty smart for a Chinaman!" Pete exclaimed.

"I'm not Chinese. My mother was Japanese, my father was an American seaman."

"Huh. Guess you are a lot taller than most of the Chinamen that used to work on the railroad. I always wondered where they all went."

"Back to China, mostly."

Jessie knew that Ki was insulted whenever anyone called him a Chinaman. When it was an intentional slight, it was cause for swift retribution, but even when unintentional, like now, it was a great source of irritation. The Japanese and Chinese had never been on good terms, and there was very little in common between them. Only the uneducated or uninformed failed to distinguish the many fundamental differences between those two ancient races and cultures.

Wanting to change the subject, Jessie said, "Which is the best hotel in town?"

"The Belmont on Main Street."

"Good. Please send Mr. Ellis there as soon as he arrives. Also, tell him that we will buy every sound mustang that he brings to us for eleven dollars a head."

"He'll like that fine. But what are you gonna do with them?"

"Hold them right here until we have an even thousand head, then ship them to Denver."

"A thousand head!" Pete said with a low whistle. "Woowee! That is one hell of a lot of mustangs. What are you doing, outfittin' an army or something?"

"Yeah," Mark said, taking Jessie's arm and cowhide suitcase. "Send Hob Ellis over to see us as soon as he comes back."

"I'll do that, young fella!" the old mustanger called to them as they headed for the center of town and the Belmont Hotel.

There was a loud banging at Jessie's door and she moved to open it. "Who's there?"

"Hob Ellis. Open up."

Jessie swung the door open and confronted a thick, smelly slab of a man. He wore a hat with a flat brim and a leather vest with a gold watch and chain. He weighed over two hundred pounds and his shoulders were so broad they filled the doorway. In his thirties, he was rough and unshaven, with a pointed jaw, hooked nose, and a three-day growth of beard. When he spoke, his voice had a raspy quality, almost like two pieces of bark being sawed against each other.

"Pete said you bought my mustangs, lady," he rumbled, his eyes moving slowly up and down her like probing fingers.

Jessie had bathed, washed her long, copper-colored hair and toweled it dry, then taken a short nap before arising to change into a fresh outfit. All the fatigue she had felt after the long train ride from Denver was gone now. She was eager to settle this business and leave Elko to catch mustangs. At this very moment, Mark and Ki were buying saddle horses, and enough food and supplies to last ten mustangers a month.

"Come inside and have a seat," Jessie told the man. "I don't discuss business in hallways."

He grunted, then clomped inside, closing the door

behind him. His face was grimy, his hands creased with dirt.

"You got anything to drink? Trail out there is mighty dusty this time of year."

Jessie splashed good sipping brandy in a glass and he tossed it down, wiped his mouth with his sleeve, and held his glass out for more.

"Good stuff!" he grunted. "You really want to buy a thousand head of mustangs?"

"Yes."

"It's too late in the year. Besides, since April I already shipped nearly that many to the slaughterhouses. The bands are almost cleaned out by now. Ain't more than a couple hundred left."

"That's not what Pete says."

The man's lip curled. "Don't listen to that old windbag. He ain't been mustanging in years! I know what I'm talking about, lady."

"I am sure you do," Jessie said, deciding that this man was crude, overbearing, and probably quick to anger. "But I intend to have the mustangs I need. My friends and I plan to go south into the central part of this state and mustang the rest of the summer. I want to know if you and your men want to hire on."

"Me? Hob Ellis work for a...a woman!" He laughed at the idea.

Jessie curbed her tongue. It would have been easy to just tell the man to get out of the room, but she knew that she needed experienced mustangers, and Hob was supposed to be the best in this area.

"I'll pay you fifty dollars a month."

"I wouldn't do it for five hundred dollars a month. Not down in the Indian country with Three Kills and his lot."

"I intend to pay him for the mustangs we take."

Hob snorted with disgust. "Lady, you go down there and he'll have that pretty hair of yours hanging from a

37

war lance. And you can guess what he'll do with you before the scalpin' starts."

Jessie ignored the lewd suggestion. "Then you refuse to help?"

Hob downed his brandy and marched across the room to grab the bottle and pour himself a full glass. He studied her for a minute before speaking. "Did Pete tell you anything about Three Kills?"

"Yes. That he was raised by missionaries and became a renegade Paiute."

"That's only part of it. Three Kills is one of the few chiefs who speaks perfect English and thinks like a military general. That Indian is crafty and fearless. Tough too! He'd as soon slit your pretty throat as . . . well, as you can guess," he said lamely, eyes dropping to the V of her tight pants as he licked his cracked lips.

Jessie's cheeks flushed with anger. "I think you have another band of horses to sell, is that correct?"

"Yeah. Seventy of 'em."

"Good. That will be seventy-seven dollars, which I will leave at the hotel desk in a sealed envelope with your name on it. I will buy any more you want to sell, as long as they are sound."

"What do you want them for?" he demanded, angry at being dismissed so summarily.

"Does it matter? Surely you have no interest in their welfare. You have been selling them to slaughterhouses, what could be worse?"

"I don't give a damn about the horses, ma'am. I just like to know the kind of a game I deal into."

"It's none of your business."

"That's where you are wrong. If you come down and start mustanging on my range, you are taking money out of my pocket. You want to buy horses from me? Fine. But stay out of the mustanging business down near the Ruby Mountains where I go. There ain't enough horses left for the both of us to make a livin' catching. You understand?"

Jessie had tried to be civil with this man, but now her temper had reached a flashpoint. He was threatening her. When someone did that, he had crossed the line.

"Mr. Ellis, I don't like threats. In fact, they make me even more determined. We have no fear of your kind, nor of the Indians." That part of it was not entirely true, but Jessie was mad and it sounded good. "I have dealt with the Comanche, Kiowa, and Apache. It's my experience that they respond to fairness. I'll pay them what I pay you."

"I ain't good at figures, lady, but I'd have to sell you ten horses to earn enough profit to offset what I lose for every horse you catch instead of me. I don't need competition, even if I thought you could catch mustangs. Smartest thing for you to do would be to load your mustangs on the next train going to wherever the hell you came from."

Jessie moved around him and pulled open the door. "Your money will be waiting at the desk below by tomorrow morning. Good evening, Mr. Ellis. Any more mustangs you catch, leave them in the shipping pens and I'll see that you are paid."

"Just who the hell are you, lady!"

"Miss Jessica Starbuck. Now get out of my room."

He shook his head and slammed the door shut, then locked it behind his back. He took the key and dropped it into his pants. "I don't think I will," he said. "I want to see the color of your money right now, and I want a little kiss to seal our deal."

Jessie backed up to her suitcase, which lay open at the foot of her bed. She should have strapped on her gun, but it was too late now. In as controlled a voice as she could muster, she said with a brittle smile, "All right, let me get your money first."

"It can wait until after we're finished," he said, coming to get her.

"No, I want to pay you first," she insisted, reaching under a jacket and sliding her long, supple fingers

39

around the polished peachwood butt of her sixgun. It had been given to her on her eighteenth birthday by her father, who had visited the Colt factory in Connecticut. Alex Starbuck had ordered Sam Colt's factory to make his daughter a special type of weapon, a one-of-a-kind that had already served her very well. It had a .44 frame but was bored and chambered for the lighter .38-caliber shells. With less recoil, Jessie could handle the gun almost as fast as a seasoned gunfighter.

"Here it is," she said, turning to discover Ellis had moved up very close and was about to put a bearhug on her. He pinned her arms to her sides and was standing so close he had not yet seen the gun. But when Jessie cocked the hammer he froze.

"Step back," she hissed.

He crushed her with a sudden, wrenching power that nearly cracked her ribs and made her faint. "Drop it or I'll squeeze the life out of you!" he snarled.

Jessie felt as if her spine was going to snap where his hands locked at the small of her back. She could not breath, and when his lips found hers and his tongue tried to force its way into her mouth, she bit him and tasted his blood.

"Ahhh!" he roared. In his pain, he forgot about her gun and released her for an instant. He raised the flat of his hand, and that's when Jessie jammed the Colt between his legs and pulled the trigger.

The muffled explosion coupled with his scream as he sprung backwards, crashed over the bed, and began to beat at the smoke emanating from the crotch of his powder-burning pants.

"Jesus Christ!" he howled. "What are you trying to do to me!"

Jessie watched him beat at himself. She guessed her bullet had not gelded the man, or he would now be completely insensible with pain. She took the bottle of brandy and walked over to pour it on the smoke. For some reason, it made Hob Ellis curl up into a ball and howl even louder.

Her door crashed open as Ki and Mark came flying into her room. Mark's gun was clenched in his fist and Ki had one of his *shuriken* star-blades poised in his hand, ready to be hurled with deadly accuracy.

"It's all right," Jessie said quickly as she motioned to Ellis. "The man was on his way out, weren't you."

He rolled to his feet, a big, mean sonofabitch who had been utterly humiliated by a woman. Jessie knew that his pride had been destroyed and that she had made a deadly enemy. But what choice had she but to defend herself from his lustful intentions? Besides, as the daughter of Alex Starbuck, she had learned that making enemies was an unavoidable fact of life. When you had something other people wanted, be it land, money, or flesh, you had to be ready to fight—and win.

"Get out of here," she said in a very soft voice. "While you still can."

Hob Ellis, bent and holding his privates, staggered to the doorway. He raised one hand and gripped the doorsill for support. "I hope to God Three Kills and his heathens torture you to death slow. And that every one of them uses you five times and—"

The *shuriken* blade sliced through the air. Had Ki wanted, he could have sent it into Ellis's throat or chest and killed the man, but instead, he used the weapon as a warning and buried it in the wood between the mustanger's index and middle fingers.

A trickle of blood smeared the painted woodwork where his hand had rested. Ellis paled, dropped his hand back to his crotch as if it had been snakebit, whirled, and bounded down the hallway.

"What the—"

Jessie cut Mark's question off with one of her own. "Did you get everything?" she asked almost matter-of-factly. "We will be leaving tomorrow."

41

"How many of us?" Ki asked, glancing back at the retreating mustanger.

"Just three." Jessie smiled. "But try to think of the bright side of things. You and Ki bought for ten, so at least we'll have plenty of food to eat."

# Chapter 4

Jessie woke very early and dressed by lamplight. She had not slept well. Over the years, she had developed an inner voice that told her when something was seriously amiss. That warning had plagued her all night long, until she had finally given up on sleep and waited until first light.

Now, she tugged on her custom-made boots and brushed her hair up on top of her head before covering it with a man's hat. She shrugged into a coat heavy enough to hide the fullness of her ample breasts and buttoned it up to the collar. And finally, she slipped the Colt revolver into her pocket and then eyed herself in the dressing mirror. *I look tired,* she thought, noticing the dark circles under her eyes. She hid her womanhood, not wanting to attract unnecessary attention. She left the room, locked it, and began to tiptoe down the hallway.

Ki stepped out behind her so quietly she was almost to the head of the stairs before he whispered, "A little early to be heading off for breakfast, isn't it?"

Jessie stopped, feeling like a child caught reaching into the cookie jar. Turning, she smiled in the dim hallway. "How did you know that I would be leaving at this hour?"

"I know you."

It was a simple statement, one which would have elicited a curious look had it not been made by this staunch protector of Jessie Starbuck and her empire. She was the power, but Ki was the everpresent steel that shielded her from harm.

And what steel he was! Orphaned very young in Japan and ostracized by the Orientals because of his mixed blood, he had almost starved to death as a child before winning himself an apprenticeship with Japan's last great samurai, the magnificent Hirata. That great man had devoted the last decade of his life to teaching Ki the profound philosophies underlying martial arts. So it was the last real master teaching the last true pupil, a completion of life's circle.

Ki had been trained in unarmed combat until he had become more deadly with hands and feet than seasoned killers were with knives and guns. Once the lessons of fighting without arms had been mastered, old Hirata had shown him how to use the bow and arrow, the sword, staff stick, and most deadly of all, the throwing weapons.

When at last Ki had mastered all these and was imbued with the spirit and clear thinking of a true samurai warrior, old Hirata had known his own life was fulfilled. He had taken it according to his ancient and honorable traditions: with a short sword he had inflicted long horizontal and vertical slashes deep into his abdomen.

Each cut had penetrated not only the body, but had even reached Hirata's soul and freed it at last. And when the great samurai had completed the ritual suicide, he had died as well as he had lived, with honor and dignity, according to his code. Ki had taken his blood-stained *katana* sword and brought it to America, where he kept it clean and razor-sharp. Only when alone did he practice with it, and then he heard the blade singing to him the whispered instruction of Hirata, telling him to be strong, to be ever vigilant and ward off all harm that might threaten the woman he had chosen to protect forever, Jessica Starbuck.

Over the years, Ki had proven himself to be not only a warrior without peer, but also the one man who could read Jessie's thoughts, sense her moods. Small wonder then that he had not slept when she had wrestled with some unknown danger.

"I should have known."

"Yes," he said in a way that held no recrimination, "but that is not important. We are going to the horses, aren't we?"

It was not a question, but a statement of fact. Jessie nodded as she started down the stairs. "I don't know what it is, but something is wrong."

As they passed the desk, she looked beyond the sleeping night clerk to the pigeonhole file where each room had a slot for messages. The envelope with Hob Ellis's money was missing. Jessie was not surprised.

Outside, they moved quickly and silently down the boardwalk. The street was deserted, except for a drunken cowboy who lay sprawled out and snoring beside a watering trough. An old black dog arose stiffly and trotted across the street to greet them with a wag of its nearly hairless tail. Jessica's fingers brushed at the animal, but she did not pause to scratch its head.

At the corner of Main and Third Streets, they heard the unmistakable sound of flesh striking flesh, and then a body slamming up against a wall.

Jessie drew her gun and began to run. Ki moved slightly ahead of her. They were approaching the deserted train station, and when they rounded it and started down the tracks toward the loading pens, they saw the cause of Jessie's inner warning.

Hob Ellis was beating the old railroad hostler, and his men looked to be getting ready to steal the mustangs. Hob had Pete up against the fence and was driving his fists into the man's face and stomach. Jessie could see that Pete was helpless, too weak to stand

45

even, so that Hob kept having to drag him up to his feet in order to hit him again.

Jessie stopped and planted her feet solidly, then drew her Colt, took aim, and fired. Her bullet sent Ellis's hat sailing into the pen of milling horses. Hob dropped the old man and whirled. When he saw Jessie and Ki, his hand stilled at his side and he froze.

"Don't shoot, Miss Starbuck! This doesn't concern you or the Chink. It's between me and the old man. Ain't that right, boys?"

The sun was just climbing into the eastern horizon and it sent an amber glow racing across the train yard, making the rails look like gold wire stretched thin and taut, running in and out of town into the long, flat distances.

"Are you all right, Pete?"

He was on the ground. Jessie could hear his tortured breathing, but he had slipped into unconsciousness.

"Pete here was going to steal a couple of your mustangs," Hob said nervously as he eyed Jessie's gun, remembering what it had almost done to him the night before. "Me and the boys just happened to be heading out when we saw him sneakin' around these pens. He's done the same to me a couple of times. Had to teach the old bastard a lesson, ma'am."

"You are a liar, Mr. Ellis," Jessie said, so furious that the gun quivered in her clenched fist. "And a bully afraid to fight someone young enough to defend himself."

The big mustang ramrod spat into the dirt. "I ain't never been afraid of fightin' no man. What's wrong with the Chink?"

"I thought you would never ask," Ki said with a murderous smile as he stepped forward.

Hob glanced at Jessie, waited for her nod of approval, then said in a triumphant voice, "Boys, watch me beat the yellow outa his hide!"

Jessie almost felt sorry for the man as Ki moved toward him, hands up, fingers stiffened. Hob threw himself off the fence and swung with a ponderous blow heavy enough to have stunned a horse.

Ki ducked under the swing and his right hand swept up in a *yonhon-nukite* spear-hand blow, rigid fingers driving into Ellis's belly, then curling as they continued their thrust upward and under the lower ribs.

Hob Ellis lifted on his toes and screamed in agony as the muscle wall of his stomach ripped like cloth. Ki's fingers bent and pulled the big man toward him.

Jessie took a sharp intake of breath, and she almost called out to Ki not to kill the mustanger. But she silenced her plea, because Ki was in a state of mind so concentrated that he heard nothing. He had already chosen not to kill Hob Ellis. Pulling him close as if Hob were helplessly impaled on a sword, Ki butted with his lower forehead. Hob's nose crunched like broken glass under a boot heel. He moaned and Ki threw him back against the fence, then whirled to face any of his friends foolish enough to interfere.

No one was that insane. They froze as their eyes tracked the downward progress of Hob when he slid to earth, then rolled over and lay convulsing on the ground.

Ki reached down for Pete and lifted him as if he were a child. Ki was slender but incredibly strong, and his movement was effortless as he walked to Jessie, then pivoted to face the mustangers.

"For now, at least, this is over," Jessie said. "Get Ellis to a doctor and stay out of our sight."

The mustangers nodded vigorously. They picked up their boss, who began to howl in pain. That set the town dogs to barking and howling too. Sleepy-eyed people pushed aside their curtains and a few even stepped outside in their nightshirts.

Jessie and Ki ignored them as they headed back to

the Belmont Hotel with Pete.

"If we leave him here," Ki observed, "he's a dead man."

"I know," Jessie replied. "But Pete figures we are also dead if we go south to mustang in Three Kills' country."

"Then I guess it shouldn't matter to him if we take him along. Either way, he has nothing to lose."

They placed Pete in the buckboard they had bought the day before and packed sacks of flour, potatoes, beans, corn, and beef jerky around him for comfort and protection. Then, with Mark and Jessie riding two new saddle horses and Ki driving two more in harness, they headed south out of Elko. It was still early morning. The day was bright and there was not a cloud in the vast blue sky.

"You should have awakened me before going down to the train yard," Mark grumbled out of injured pride. "I could have helped."

"I know that. Ki said the same to me."

"You mean you were going out there alone?"

Jessie nodded. "Feels good to be astride a horse again, doesn't it, Mark? Why don't we just think about what lies ahead and enjoy the morning together?"

He flushed with irritation. "No man can tell you anything, can they?"

"Nope."

Mark cussed. "I never met the likes of you before and sometimes, like right now, I hope to never meet the likes of you again!"

She laughed, the sound of it open and infectious enough to dispel his anger. "Don't say that yet, Mark. You still have no idea what you're missing."

"What does that mean?" he asked with sudden interest.

She looked at him and said with total candor, "I'm not yet sure myself."

Mark opened his mouth, then seemed to change his

mind and clamped it shut again. Maybe he realized that there might not be a great deal of time left in the world for any of them. Up against a band of renegade Indians, even Ki with all his skills and strange weapons would not stand the chance of a snowball in hell.

The Ruby Mountains were the only things green for as far as Jessie could see. This northeastern Nevada reminded her somewhat of the Big Bend country of Texas. It was high, rugged, and empty until you really began to study it closely.

"You see that high mesa over yonder?" Pete asked. "I named it Fire's Last Stand."

"Why?" Jessie asked, staring at the face of a cliff that dropped a good hundred and fifty feet into a jumble of rocks below.

"Ten years ago there was a stallion named Fire that no one could catch. Finest-looking sonofabitch you ever laid eyes upon. He was a liver chestnut. Red and faster than a high Kansas wind. There was a thousand-dollar reward for the man who could catch him. I tried two years before I finally trapped that devil up on the edge of the mesa."

Pete squinted his eyes and seemed to look back in time. "There was me, Ed Bostic, Shorty Best, and Chet Sampson. We ran the stallion and his mares up on that mesa and when they reached the cliff, we was so damned excited we could almost start spending our money.

"But Fire knew he was trapped. He saw the ropes in our hands and figured it was all over. So he just whirled away and jumped."

Jessie blinked. "You mean off the cliff?"

"That's right. Fire made up his mind that he would rather be dead than roped and corralled. Some men are that way, they'd rather be shot or hung than face life in prison."

Pete shook his head, the pain of that day still very

49

much a part of him. "I almost quit mustanging for good after that. And I damn sure never trapped no wild stallions up on no high mesa again."

On the second day out, they came across three dead stallions. When Pete rode up to stare down at them, anger flashed in his eyes.

"They were bachelors," he explained. "Two of them were young stallions not quite full-growed enough to challenge for a band of mares. The third, that bay, was old. Probably lost his own band of mares in the last few years to a younger stud. All horses like company and you'll seldom see one alone. The bachelors watch out for each other, but there ain't a mustang alive that can outrun a rifle's bullet."

Jessie shook her head. "Gelded, the young ones would have made fine riding horses."

"Sure they would have," Pete said loudly, "but they'd have been a lot harder to catch, so they was shot instead."

"Hob Ellis?"

"Probably. Though ranchers in this part of the country shoot 'em as quick as they would a coyote." Pete looked away, his face set hard and grim. "Let's get out of here. We still got a ways to go."

Slowed by the buckboard, they traveled for two more days. The land grew tougher, the grass harder to find, and the pines more stunted and wind-bent. But whenever they came to a spring or one of the creeks that tumbled off the Ruby Mountains, they saw that the mud was churned by increasing numbers of mustangs.

Late one afternoon, they topped a treeless ridge and stared down into a wide valley. "See that clump of cottonwood trees?" Pete barked.

They nodded.

"That is a prime watering hole, and the place where we'll catch our mustangs."

His thick finger traced the ridges and contours of the land. "What we want is a natural kind of funnel we can drive the mustangs through. This valley narrows toward the spring. It's as pretty a setup for mustanging as you'd ever hope to find."

Jessie nodded. "Then let's get at it."

They had built a stout corral around the spring. Jessie had used an ax to trim the branches from two felled cottonwoods while Mark and Ki had done the tough work of splitting them for posts and rails. Almost every post hole had been dug only after hours of backbreaking labor, for the ground was filled with rocks.

But now, as they sweated under a late-afternoon sun and finished hanging the big gate in place, they each had a deep sense of satisfaction. The corral itself was about a hundred feet in diameter and a good eight feet tall. Where possible, they had used upstanding cottonwood trees whose strength lent support to the entire corral. None of them figured it was a work of art, but Pete said it was a "good 'un," and that meant a lot.

That night they were optimistic and eager to begin mustanging until Pete said, "Well, we did the first half of the thing right nicely. Tomorrow we'll start on the wings. Another week ought to do 'er just fine."

This announcement was about as welcome as a skunk at a church social. Pete shrugged helplessly. "Without wings fannin' out from the gate, there ain't a chance in hell of driving a band of mustangs into this corral."

"How long and high do they have to be?"

"About two hundred feet long, hundred across the opening."

"Damnation!" Mark snorted. "It'll take us another two weeks."

But Pete shook his head and explained that since the wings were used only to direct the mustangs, they did not need to be very strong. "Long as they stand up in a

51

light breeze, they'll do fine. Only have to be about four feet tall. Posts will go in half as deep as the ones we used in the corral."

Ki rolled up in his blankets without a word, and that was a signal for the rest of them to get some sleep. The hard work wasn't finished yet. They were still not ready to do the actual job of mustanging.

Jessie, Mark, and Ki worked like Roman slaves to build the wings quickly. Pete would not allow them to cut down any more of the cottonwoods for fear the sight would spook the mustangs too much and make them impossible to drive toward the corral. That meant that they had to take the buckboard up into the hills and cut down the tough, bushy piñon and juniper pine and spend hours trimming away branches to get enough solid trunk for posts and rails.

Pete had recovered enough to begin to ride out every morning into the nearby hills in search of mustangs. Each morning he headed off in a different direction and when Jessie asked him why, he explained the mustangs were territorial.

"The stallion of one band can't hardly be driven by man across that of another stallion," he explained. "Once you figure out where their boundaries are, then you can begin to see how you can drive them into those wings."

They had a drenching cloudburst on the day they finished the wings. Jessie, Ki, and Mark stood with their faces turned upward to the sky and let the rain wash away the accumulated dust and sweat. They finished setting the last poles and then hiked up to a high piece of ground and stared down at the results of their labors.

"We did a damned good job," Mark said.

Ki nodded. "I hope Pete hasn't any more late surprises for us. Compared to pounding out post holes and chopping timber, the mustanging itself is going to seem like a vacation."

52

Jessie agreed. The rain had left the hills smelling fresh and the sage had a spicy pungency that was almost heady. Their corral appeared formidable and from a distance the wings looked perfectly straight and very strong. These past two weeks had been physically demanding, but she and the others had thrived. Jessie could not remember when she had ever felt fitter, and had it not been for the urgency of their mission plus the constant worry they had of being surprised by Three Kills and his Indians, it would have been a very good time.

"Here comes the boss," Jessie said with a smile.

They watched Pete come galloping into view. He sat his horse like he was a part of the animal and had the carriage and look of a young man. Pete galloped his horse down through the wings and into the corral. He circled it, and Jessie knew his eyes were measuring every foot of rail and gauging the strength of each of the posts. Twice, he cantered around the corral before reining his horse back into the wings and then coming up to join them.

When he stopped his winded horse, he pushed back his Stetson and said, "Tomorrow, we go mustanging. But first, I reckon it only fair to tell you that I've seen signs of Indians out yonder."

Jessie swallowed dryly. This was the news they had been dreading, yet had expected. This country was huge and lonesome, but Indians always seemed to sense when their territory was being trespassed upon.

"How many?" Ki asked.

"About six." Pete gestured to the southwest. "They watched us for a couple of days, then took off. Probably went to get some friends."

"Chief Three Kills?" Jessie asked.

"I reckon."

Jessie looked to Mark, then to Ki. "What do you think? If you want to leave now, I won't argue."

Ki stepped forward. "Do you want to leave, Jessie?"

"No," she said. "We've put too much time and work into this to quit now."

"Jessie, I could trail them and see if I can—"

Jessie shook her head. "No, Ki. We stay together. If we have to fight, at least we might have a chance that way."

They nodded in agreement.

They awoke hours before sunrise and downed a quick breakfast of coffee and cold meat. Pete, Mark, and Jessie had decided to locate the mustangs and drive them down the valley toward the corral where Ki would be hiding.

"Your job," Pete told Ki, "is to dig a hole just big enough to crouch in and hide. Cover yourself up with a piece of brush and, after the mustangs come thundering into the corral, jump up and close the gate. It's heavy and you'll have to be very fast. Once the stallion realizes there is only one way out, he'll come storming back toward that gate and hit it like a train. If it isn't barred, it will knock you down and the whole bunch will come streaking out."

"I understand."

"Good," Pete said. "You got the toughest and most dangerous part. All we have to do is ride like bats outa hell. I seen more than one good man trampled to death trying to close a mustang catch-corral gate."

The martial-arts master flexed his limber muscles. Jessie had no doubts at all that he could handle the gate, despite the fact that it was extremely heavy and cumbersome. As she rode away, she waved back to Ki, but he did not see her because he was already furiously digging his hiding place.

It felt wonderful to be astride a horse again and galloping like a free spirit across the land. The sun was coming up and the silhouettes of the hills, mountains, trees, and ridges loomed out of the fading darkness. An hour later Pete suddenly swung his horse off to the left and indicated for them to peel away to the right and follow a cut in the hills.

Jessie felt her heart beat faster. Stirrup to stirrup she galloped beside Mark, who rode beautifully, his back straight, his strong horseman's legs gripping his mount expertly. He kept looking sideways at her, face alive with his own keen excitement. He was handsome and fresh-looking despite the hard work of two weeks. Jessie had never felt a stronger sense of the sheer joy of being alive. Danger always gave life its sharpest edge, etched every moment indelibly in one's mind.

"Look!" Mark called. "Down in that gully and along that hillside!"

Jessie saw them. A huge band of mustangs, just now snapping their heads up. A magnificent chestnut stallion trumpeted a call of warning and lunged into the midst of his mares. He started to drive them away, and that was when Pete seemed to rise up out of the earth and fire his gun.

The chestnut changed directions and slammed back into his confused band of mares. Jessie and Mark reined hard and came barreling down a steep slope, waving their hats and shouting at the top of their lungs.

"Ya!" Mark shouted hoarsely. "Yip-ya!"

The stallion had no choice but to drive his mares in the only path of escape. And to Jessie's delight, it was going to lead them straight back to the wings and their brand-new catch corral.

"Woowee!" she cried, urging her horse into a dead run as they hit flat ground and chased after the racing mustangs. Mustanging was even more exciting than she had thought it would be.

But then, the glint of sun on steel winked from a distant ridge and caught Jessie's eye. She stared hard through the churning dust and saw Indians. They were coming fast from the south. Jessie's hand moved reassuringly toward the butt of her sixgun. It was too late to run from the Indians.

*To hell with it,* she thought, *let's catch the mustangs and then let the chips fall where they may!*

"Woowee-yip!" she yelled, to the rolling thunder of hoofbeats.

# Chapter 5

She could only see seven Indians, and that worried her more than anything. Where were the others? Had they killed Ki and lain in ambush at the catch corral? A hundred fears sprung to Jessie's mind as they raced after the band of mustangs. Her apprehension intensified because the Indians were not trying to catch them, but were obviously going to allow them to finish the mustang roundup. *They must have laid a trap for us up ahead*, she thought grimly.

Dust boiled into the cloudless sky and the ground shook. Jessie's mind was going sixteen ways to sundown as she tried to think of what was going to happen after they corralled these mustangs. Would the Indians attack, or just demand the horses? Would they listen and bargain, or simply take what they wanted—including scalps?

"Watch the stallion!" Pete shouted.

The chestnut was trying to drive his mares up a side gully, but Mark Lyon was ready. His lariat streaked out and caught the big horse, and then Mark roughly turned his back.

Ahead loomed the wings of the corral, looking like a pair of lover's arms opened wide. The mustangs tried once more to veer away when they saw the strange wings, but their momentum carried them onward. Now they were inside the wings and thundering toward the corral.

Jessie looked for a sign of Ki and found none. She glanced back toward the Indians, but they were temporarily blocked from sight by a low seam of land. Where were the rest of the Indians hiding?

The mustangs were running hard—ears back, nostrils red and distended, lungs burning for air. Jessie estimated there were at least eighty, possibly more, and that all but the colts and fillies would make suitable mounts for President González's army. But with the Indians in pursuit, Mexico and the revolutionaries they were trying to prevent from taking control of that country seemed as if they were from another space and time.

"Yee-yip!" Mark bellowed and was answered in turn by the old mustanger, as the band exploded through the catch-corral gate.

Jessie almost laughed with happiness when she saw Ki spring from the earth and hurl himself at the gate. The Indians had not yet had time to spring their own trap!

· The chestnut stallion hit the far side of their corral fence and rebounded with unbelievable quickness. Ki slammed down the heavy bar that secured the gate just a heartbeat before the stallion struck with the full force of his body.

Wood splintered, and Jessie held her breath for an instant. The stallion reeled back as Ki waved a horse blanket at its face. The animal lunged a second time and the gate bent like a bow. A rail cracked like a buffalo rifle. The stallion fell back, then threw itself at the gate once more. Its head shot through the hole where the rail had splintered and its teeth snapped at Ki's body. Ki dodged those vicious teeth, grabbed the splintered rail, and shoved it back in place.

Now Mark and Pete were flying off their sliding horses and throwing their bodies at the gate to lend Ki support. The furious stallion whirled and went kicking and biting into his band of churning mares.

58

"We did it!" Pete shouted, but his voice went flat and small as he looked back toward where the Indians would appear any moment. "This is one of the finest bands of horses I ever caught in one bunch. Think we can trade them for our lives?" It was a poor joke, and now Mark and Jessie were pulling out their Winchester rifles and levering in shells.

Ki moved quickly to their camp and returned a moment later with his bow and quiver of arrows. He did not watch for the Indians, but fixed all his attention on the task at hand. Having had to wait so long in the hole he had dug, he had chosen to be shirtless and now, as he carefully strung the bow with a fine gut string, the perfect symmetry of his torso was revealed. Ki was smooth-muscled, like a racehorse rather than a draft animal. His biceps did not bulge and yet there was a cat-like strength that was evident in the way his shoulders and chest were formed. His bow was unlike anything seen in the West. It was about five feet long, with several strange-looking knots and curves in it. When Ki gripped the weapon, it was not in the center, but instead a third of the way up from the bottom. He selected an arrow from the quiver and nocked it, then waited, his face impassive, his eyes as cold as stone.

The Indians appeared at the crest of the hill. "It's him," Pete said. "I never saw Three Kills, but I know he's a big bastard and he rides a black-and-white spotted Appaloosa stallion."

When the Indians reached the head of the wings, they reined in and waited as their chief urged his stallion forward. Ki was startled at the resemblance he saw between Three Kills and his old samurai teacher, Hirata. Like that great Japanese warrior, Three Kills was mountainous, with a massive pair of shoulders and arms thick with muscle. He was not a young man. His long black hair was heavily streaked with gray and his face was deeply creased by sun and wind. In addition to his size,

Three Kills had that immense presence that could not be taught or faked, but only came from years of suffering and great wisdom. Ki relaxed. This man was so like Hirata he knew before a word was spoken that Three Kills was neither bloodthirsty nor vicious. As the Paiute chief neared him, Ki now saw that the Indian's eyes pierced a man's mind and heart like the obsidian points of war arrows.

Ki stepped out to meet the Indian chief, saying, "All of you stay back and let me talk to him quietly."

Mark protested, but Jessie grabbed his arm. "Don't let your pride overrule good sense. The man is coming alone; he expects to be met by one we consider nearest his equal."

Mark slowly relaxed and Jessie knew that he was under control and would not act foolishly. As for Pete, he also seemed relaxed, until you noticed how white his knuckles were where he gripped his rifle.

Ki, with his deadly war bow in hand, moved halfway out to the center of the wings before coming to a standstill. Jessie could not help but compare him with the Indian. Lithe and slender, Ki appeared like a boy next to the thick-chested Paiute who dismounted and stepped forward. And yet, she knew with certainty that Ki was more than the physical equal of Three Kills and, if they fought, the martial-arts master would emerge the victor.

"Who are you?" Three Kills asked in such surprisingly good English that even Ki might have been shocked had he not heard Pete detail this chief's unusual missionary upbringing.

"My name is Ki. I am friend and protector of Miss Jessica Starbuck. We come in peace."

The Indian's face displayed immense disgust. "You are not a white man, why do you lie like one?"

"I am half Japanese, half white. I am a warrior like yourself, but trained in different ways."

Three Kills was not impressed. He studied Ki's

strange-looking bow and then looked back into his eyes. "I could grab you by the throat and end your life with a twist," Three Kills said quietly.

Ki stood impassively. He knew how important face was to leaders of men, and he had no doubt that Three Kills was challenging his courage. The trick, he decided, was to let this chief know that he was not being intimidated and yet not to fight to the death. Ki wished he could look about and locate the rest of the Indians who were out there somewhere, probably with their rifle sights trained on Jessie.

"You are strong enough to kill me," Ki agreed, choosing his words as carefully as a jeweler might a selection of diamonds. "But I am strong enough to also kill. There is no need for death songs among our peoples. The wind blows warm in your land, can it not also whisper into our minds words of reason and peace?"

Three Kills' eyes drew down to slits. "You come to this land from across the sea and steal our horses. Do you expect me to allow you to take them and go away?"

"No," Ki said. "We will pay you well for the horses —if you help us catch more."

His proposal was audacious, daring, and totally spontaneous. Ki had not intended to ask for Three Kills' help, but now that the words were spoken, he did not regret them. They badly needed help and maybe these Indians did too.

Three Kills was caught off guard. "You steal our horses, then demand our help!"

"Not steal, buy. There are too many for your warriors. The horses are thin and the grass is withered and brown. Trade horses for money. Your people need food, new hunting weapons and ammunition. Am I wrong, Chief Three Kills?"

During a long, brooding silence, Ki thought he might have crossed that boundary from which there was no escape except in death. To suggest to this proud chief

61

that his people needed help was the height of boldness, perhaps even insanity. And yet, something inside Ki told him this chief was reasonable, wise, and fair. Even more important, Ki guessed that Three Kills' people were hungry, almost to the point of starvation. The Paiute chief himself was thirty pounds too light and his warriors were in equally poor condition. Their ribs could be counted and there was a feverish look to their faces that said they had not eaten in days.

Most of them were armed with bows and arrows like himself, but some carried old flintlock rifles that were now considered relics. These Indians would stand no chance at all in a skirmish with the United States Cavalry. Despite their bloody reputation in Elko, they appeared to Ki more desperate than dangerous. Ki wondered if his other warriors, the women, and the children were also in such bad shape.

Three Kills looked back toward his men and seemed to realize it would be ridiculous to deny their pathetic circumstances. And yet, pride kept him from accepting the proposal.

"We do not need your help in catching wild horses," he said with his head held proudly.

"I know that, but we do need yours. Chief, we must have one thousand mustangs before the snow falls. We will pay you fairly."

"How?" Three Kills challenged him with the question. It was certain he believed Ki would attempt to cheat him and his people.

Ki turned to beckon Jessie, Mark, and Pete to join him. "I have told Chief Three Kills we are willing to pay his people well for the horses we take, but we need their help in catching and driving them to Elko."

"No!" the chief said harshly. "We cannot go to Elko. Whites will kill us."

"You don't need to come all the way," Jessie said quickly. "Just close enough so that we can get them into the railroad pens."

62

A second Indian had joined the chief and he said something in their language. The man was tall and would have been handsome had it not been for a crooked nose and an ugly saber scar across one cheek. They began to argue. Once, the Indian pointed at Ki's oddly shaped bow and gesticulated in anger.

Chief Three Kills finally silenced the man with an angry word that left them both quivering with unconcealed fury.

"This is Bloody Knife. He is a Shoshone who left his own people when his chief agreed to a treaty and a reservation," the Paiute chief said to Ki. "He wanted to know why I didn't take the horses and kill you without any more talk. When I told him you would pay us in gold, he said you lie. That your tongue is as crooked as your bow."

"Tell him I speak straight and tell the truth," Ki said.

The two Indians talked again, quieter this time, but with rapid and swift hand movements that told Ki better than words this pair was still in sharp disagreement. Ki wondered why Three Kills even listened to the man, who obviously hated whites and wanted to kill them. Finally, Three Kills turned almost wearily back to Ki.

"He still says you are lying. He challenges you to prove your words are not as crooked as your bow."

"Agreed," Ki said, happy to settle the issue in any way they saw fit. He renocked his arrow with a half smile and began to speak to no one in particular. "High up in the cottonwood tree, directly behind where I stand, there is the nest of a raven. If you look closely, you will see that the bird has found a piece of glittering metal. It is Indian jewelry and it is tangled in the branches. Look closely and you will see it."

"There." Mark pointed. "I see it now! It must be sixty feet up and . . . hell, I couldn't hit it with a sixgun from this distance."

Ki waited until they were all looking at the object— even the other Indians, though they did not understand.

Then he whirled and drew back the bowstring in a single motion. His eyes lifted high into the branches of the tree. His bowstring hummed with menace as the arrow launched itself into a sharp climb at a velocity that no Indian had ever witnessed or believed possible. The arrow punctured the shiny piece of metal and ripped it from the branches. Arrow and jewelry plummeted to earth.

Everyone except Jessie, who had often seen Ki's amazing feats of accuracy with his weapon, was astonished.

"Jesus!" whispered Mark.

"Sonofabitch," said Pete, who kept staring up at the now-empty branches as if disbelieving his own eyes.

But it was Three Kills himself who gave Ki the greatest accolade when he shook his big head and grunted, "Damn good shooting."

Bloody Knife alone seemed upset as he went to retrieve the jewelry and arrow. It was a girl's silver pendant with an eagle and snake engraved on one side and a bird on the other. Its beaten silver was very thin and Ki's arrow had pierced it exactly in the center. Ki retrieved the pendant from Bloody Knife while the man began to argue vehemently with Three Kills.

"What is wrong now?" Ki asked.

"He says it was a lucky shot."

Ki's expression hardened with impatience. He handed the pendant to Three Kills and said, "I will bet you those horses against your help that I can put an arrow through it before it touches the earth again."

"No one could do such a thing."

"I can. Throw it as high as you can, Chief," he said, nocking his bow with a second arrow.

The big Paiute nodded and hurled the pendant toward the sun. It wasn't fair, because the shining silver was blinding his eyes, but Ki waited until it was low against the hills, then allowed his mind to see the target. Then he simply allowed the bow and arrow to do the work for which they were made. A thousand hours had been spent in concentrated practice when he was a very young man. During all those hours, he had never once fired, but simply imagined how he would draw the bow and send his arrow winging swiftly to its target, no matter how far or small that target might be. Hirata had taught him that with the proper mind there was literally no possibility of missing.

Ki unleashed the arrow he had selected from among a varied assortment in his quiver. This one had a wedge-shaped head of steel with serrated edges. It made a slight whistling sound as it soared across the thin, high-desert air and then, to the total amazement of everyone, sheared the pendant in two.

"My God!" Mark cried. "How did it—"

"The arrow," Ki said, explaining to them all, "is called the 'cleaver' in Japan. It is used to sever the bonds of a friend, an enemy's battle flag, or lines with hooks used by the enemy to pull themselves up into a fortress."

This time it was Three Kills who went to fetch the pendant. He walked back slowly, his thumb touching the razor-sharp serrations in wonder. He shook his head in unconcealed amazement. When he reached them, he said, "If we help, will you teach me how to do this?"

Ki smiled. "I will try. But it is an art that takes many years of study and practice."

Three Kills handed the pendant back to Ki and said a very strange thing. "Then never mind. My people and I do not expect to live very much longer."

He looked away toward the mountains. "How much will you pay for our horses?"

"Ten dollars each," Jessie said.

"That is twice what we have ever been paid before."

"Ten dollars," Jessie repeated. "In gold. All together, that adds up to—"

"I know what it adds up to," the Paiute said quietly. "I am not stupid."

"I never suggested you were. I apologize if it sounded that way."

Because it was clear that Jessie had not intended to slight him in any way, Three Kills relaxed, then pointed back to the tall cottonwoods. "On the highest branches, the leaves will soon start to turn yellow. There is much work to do and little time before the snow falls. We will help you."

The Shoshone named Bloody Knife must have known enough English to understand, because his lip curled and he spun around and marched stiffly away.

"Do not turn your back on him," Three Kills warned them. "His father was killed by the whites many years ago and he has never forgotten his pledge of vengeance."

"Why do you keep him among you?" Ki dared to ask.

"Because he is brave and will fight to save our women and children. Because my daughter, Chena, aches for the pain and anger he carries inside. And also because he has nowhere else to go."

The chief abruptly turned away and mounted his Appaloosa stallion. Without a backward glance he drummed the heels of his mocassins into the ribs of the horse and galloped away.

Pete expelled a deep sigh of relief. "I hope we never see him and his bloodthirsty bunch again," he declared. "I'll take our chances alone."

But Ki shook his head. "He is a good man, one who needs our money very much, or he would never allow us to buy the horses."

"How many warriors will he return with?" Mark asked. "Maybe it's a trick. Maybe he just wants us to catch a few more bands, and then they will attack in force and try to take everything."

Jessie glanced at Ki and then back toward the receding horsemen. "Ki believes he is a man of his word and so do I. We will trust him—but not the one called Bloody Knife."

"All right," Mark said, his voice carrying a warning, "but you had better believe that Three Kills did not come by his name just for killing three ground squirrels."

They caught two more bands of mustangs, but they were small. By the time the Indians returned, they still had only about a hundred potential army mounts for the president of Mexico. No one had to tell Jessie that they were facing an almost impossible task in trying to meet such a huge order so quickly. Circle Star ranch could, of course, glean a hundred or so from its own herds if necessary, and Mark had already suggested that he and his father could supply about fifty good horses from their remuda. Others could be bought from the Cheyenne, Salt Lake City, and Denver stockyards, but they would have to be purchased in small numbers to avoid attracting attention. Also, ranch horses were branded, and that would create more problems.

They were invited by Three Kills to visit the Indian camp, but Pete would hear nothing of that idea. He mistrusted the offer.

"Go ahead, join them heathen for supper and find yourself the meat in their pot!" he ranted. "But don't expect to find me here when you come back scalped!"

Jessie smiled because that made no sense at all. Someone was needed to watch the horses. They had begun to build more corrals and Pete seemed content to work away on them while they were gone.

Jessie was not sure what she expected when they topped a rise and looked down upon the Indian camp. She had never dealt with Paiutes but suspected that they, like most southwestern tribes, did not have the animal skins to construct tepees and so built hogans or mud-covered huts.

But when she gazed down on the village, what she saw was a pitiful collection of canvas lean-tos and several shelters built of nothing but rock and brush. And instead of a big camp, this one was extremely small. She saw no more than a dozen thin children and perhaps twice that many adults, many of them very old.

Jessie looked sideways at Ki and she could tell by his reaction that he was also shocked at the condition of these people. The warriors who rode with Three Kills were obviously the only men fit to hunt.

At their arrival, the children smiled and laughed, but the old women looked away, haunted eyes filled with hatred and mistrust. The young boys all stared at Ki and his bow and arrows, which they had obviously heard about. Ki pretended not to notice. He was not a man who enjoyed being the center of attention.

Dogs barked, horses snorted, and the children ran naked. Three Kills had chosen his campsite some five miles away from their own. A weak spring trickled into the brush-covered hillside and bled down into a swale where there was a light green blush of grass.

Ki leaned over toward Jessie and Mark. "From the talk in Elko, you'd have thought there were a thousand renegade Indians ready to sweep away every town between Salt Lake City and the California border. These people aren't doing anything but trying to exist."

Three Kills dismounted and a very pretty young maiden that Ki guessed was his daughter, Chena, came forward to tether his stallion. She was tall like her father, but had none of his heavy features. The most striking thing about her was that she was extremely light-skinned, and her nose and cheekbones were unlike those of any Indian that Ki had ever seen before. It occurred to him at once that this girl, who could not have been over eighteen, was a halfbreed. She too was thin, and because they were both of mixed races, Ki's sympathy went out to her at once, though his expression gave no indication of his feelings.

The chief indicated that they were to leave their horses to the women and join him under a ragged canvas. In a few minutes, Chena returned and began to prepare the meal. It would be some kind of rabbit soup, very long on the soup and short on the rabbit from the looks of it, Ki thought.

For a moment, his eyes touched those of the girl. He wanted to tell her that everything was going to become better for her father and his people. That they would soon have money from the horses to buy food, even if he had to do the buying himself. The rains surely must come with the fall weather, and then the land would sprout new life. Deer and antelope might once again forage and grow sleek and fat.

Ki smiled and Chena returned his smile shyly. Her round dark eyes were a reflection of his own. But suddenly, those eyes shuttered out the warmth, and Ki saw apprehension touch them for an instant.

He twisted around to see Bloody Knife standing in the doorway, his mouth curled into a mixture of hate and contempt. Chena stared down at the pot of rabbit soup and stirred quickly. Bloody Knife said something to her father and then stormed away to march out to the horses, mount, and gallop off.

"Where is he going?" Ki asked softly.

"To hunt. He says he must hunt to fill the bellies of the whites."

Ki nodded in silence. After they ate, he was determined that he would take his bow and do a little hunting of his own.

# Chapter 6

Three Kills seemed a softer, almost gentle kind of man once Bloody Knife and his warriors were out of sight. After Chena poured them soup in wooden bowls, the Paiute chief ate sparingly, and Ki knew that it was because there was so little to share.

In his small brush shelter, Ki saw books. His surprise must have been evident, because Three Kills said, "Yes, I can read, too, and so can Chena. Her mother made me promise to raise her in the Indian world, but also to teach her to speak and read English."

Jessie glanced at the girl, then back to her father. "You are both quite remarkable. May I ask what happened to Chena's mother?"

"After I ran away from the missionaries as a very young man, I lived alone in the desert for many years. I was Indian, but raised as a white, and I had to find my own *karma*."

Ki smiled. The man was obviously very well-read, for few Americans understood that term to mean the totality of one's actions in life, which determines his past, present, and future. "That is not a Christian term," he said with a curious smile.

The Paiute looked directly at him. "I was taught by the Catholic missionaries about Jesus and His Father. I believe in such a man and yet I know that the source of all things can be many things to many people. To the Indian, the sun and the moon are gods. Who would argue that they are not either gods, or things created by God, and that it is all together and in one presence?"

"Well spoken," Ki said. "I agree. It is useless and even contrary to the teachings of all religions to quibble and kill in the name of one belief as opposed to another."

The chief nodded. "You are wise."

"Tell them about my mother," Chena whispered with girlish impatience.

Three Kills continued with his story. "When I was twenty-five, I came upon a prospector and his wife who had been shot for their gold and left for dead in a mine. The young woman, whose name I learned to be Rebecca, was yet alive. She had been . . . used and when I first touched her and she saw me, she could not silence her own screams. I stayed near, left food and water at her side. After she had grown stronger, the men came back."

The Paiute took a clay pipe and filled it with something that was like tobacco but had a sharper aroma when smoked. He told his story slowly. "We were in the mine and I had only a bow and arrows, and not much food or water. When night came, I left the mine and found them in the darkness. I killed them with my knife, one by one."

"And there were three," Ki said. "And that is how you got your name."

"Yes. I tried to take Rebecca back to her people but she . . ." Three Kills hesitated, searching without success for the right words to use.

Jessie guessed the reason for his discomfort was modesty. "She had fallen in love with you. It is not so hard to understand."

Three Kills nodded. "Yes. We were married in the Indian way and she melted the stone that had become my heart. For five years, all was good for us and for all the Paiute people. The rains were plentiful, there were

71

many deer and bighorn sheep in the mountains. But always, we have been a people who lived on the harvest of pine nuts. Chena and a brother was born. Then many whites came seeking gold and silver beneath the earth. They chopped down the trees and buried them beneath the ground in their mines, and soon there were no pine nuts to harvest. That winter the sun god left his people and two hundred Paiutes died of hunger and freezing. Chena's mother and brother were among them."

"I am sorry."

Three Kills choked with anger. "It is too late to be sorry. You see how many are left now. The others have gone to the reservation." He stabbed the earth with a thick forefinger. "But this is our home until the evil whites realize we are weak and have only a few guns. When they know we cannot defend our land, they will come again and kill. That is why you must take Chena and our women and children when you leave with the horses."

"No, Father!" The young woman came to his side. "Please. I would die rather than leave you and this land."

"You are half white," he said. "Maybe they will treat you better than the Indian."

"But—"

"Silence," he said in a voice that was not loud, but had all the finality of a bullet. "You will obey me. It has been decided."

Chena twisted around and her eyes searched for help.

"It does not have to end that way," Jessie said.

"You do not understand."

"You are right," she answered. "I can't understand because, unlike you or Ki, I have never known bad treatment because of the color of my skin or the shape of my nose or eyes. But I do understand politics and power. And I believe that I can help you and these poor people."

72

"Make no promises," Three Kills said.

"All right, but I can say that, with the mustang money you will get for helping us, you can buy thousands of acres—enough to keep your people and all the ones that will come."

"The Indian is not allowed to buy land!"

"They do in New Mexico," Mark said. "They own title."

Three Kills learned forward on his haunches. "This is true?"

"Yes," Mark continued, excited with the idea of helping these people. "My father is a friend of the President of the United States. If you help us get those mustangs, the President will be very grateful."

"Your father will speak to him?"

"I'm sure of it!"

"And I will too," Jessie said. "You see, while my father lived, he became a very important man, with many friends in power. Among them is Carl Schurz, Secretary of the Interior. I have known him since I was just a little girl, when he was a frequent guest to our ranch."

Three Kills did not smile or in any way indicate the hope that blossomed in his great chest. Instead, he stood and walked to his doorway, where he surveyed his desperate little following. "We will do these things together," he said in a strong, decisive voice. "For like the mustang we hunt to keep from starvation this winter, there is nowhere else for my people to go."

He turned around. "What do you want these horses for?"

Jessie explained. When she was finished, Three Kills nodded. "Tomorrow we will begin the hunting. You have brought hope to my heart."

It had been impossible to slip away quietly, but Ki had left the Paiute camp attracting as little attention as possi-

73

ble. He was sure there were deer high up in the distant Ruby Mountains, but these people needed food now, so he would hunt rabbit.

He thought of his old teacher, Hirata, who would have been incensed that he would condescend to hunt such lowly creatures. Ki did not agree. When a warrior or his people were hungry, there was nothing shameful about keeping the body alive until a worthy target could be found. But when Ki looked back, he remembered that he had disagreed very little with his old samurai mentor and friend. Only once had their wills clashed. It had been a matter of Ki's refusal to carry the *katana,* the ritual samurai sword. Hirata had insisted that the sword was a warrior's spiritual link to his past.

Ki had dared to refuse, saying, "I am unworthy, master. I will use the bow, the knife, and the small but deadly *shuriken* star-blades, because I am most certainly not of noble birth."

Ki pulled his thoughts back to the present and walked into the nearby hills to hunt. He chose an arrow best suited for killing rabbit, then bent to study the tracks in the brush. His eyes searched the dry ground and found the tracks of sage hens, rabbits, mice, a snake, and soon even a desert tortoise. He followed the tortoise track until he overtook the heavy and ponderous creature. Ki drew his *tanto* knife from its sheath and crept forward. The tortoise did not see Ki's shadow or hear the sound of his feet, he moved so stealthily. With his incredibly fast hands, Ki had no trouble reaching out and snatching the tortoise by the throat before it could retract into its shell.

The tortoise was very strong. Its beaklike mouth opened and closed soundlessly as it struggled to free itself. Ki hesitated. He did not know if Paiutes ate tortoise, and this one seemed very old and was probably tough. Again and again the creature tried to bite his hand and Ki admired its courage. Finally, he laid the tortoise back on its feet and let it scramble into the brush. Though the Japanese loved sea turtle and considered it a delicacy, they also considered it a very special creature possessing great dignity. Ki decided that perhaps its desert cousin should be spared. Besides, a rabbit possessed little dignity and would not be so stringy. Ki harbored no doubts he could kill many rabbits before darkness.

The first one he saw was hopping through the brush fifty yards from where he stood. Ki's body seemed to blend into his surroundings as he drew his arrow back past his ear. The smooth muscles of his arms knotted. It took tremendous strength to draw the bow and hold it statuelike. Ki knew he had to time his arrow perfectly and let it thread itself between clumps of sage across a distance of fifty yards. The arrow passed with swift and deadly silence to the heart of the rabbit. The animal died instantly and Ki slung its warm, quivering body from a leather string that hung from his waistband. Within twenty minutes, he had shot two more rabbits and a sage hen. Ki judged that he had another hour before darkness. With luck, he hoped to double his kill and return to the Paiutes with enough meat to feed the camp well.

His hunt had carried him toward their own mustanging camp and when he came upon the tracks of an unshod Indian pony, Ki might have thought nothing of it, except the horse droppings were still fresh and slick. Ki paused to think about that. He studied the tracks once more and decided that, from their depth and placement, this was not just another mustang. It was being ridden with deliberate purpose through the sagebush. His eyes followed the tracks and they led directly toward the catch corral where Pete had remained to guard their mustangs.

Ki frowned. Ahead of him lay a shelf of rocks, and he knew he would be able to see his camp from that vantage point. He decided it would be worth using a few precious minutes of the fading light to assure himself that all was well.

The rocks were tall and still warm from the hottest part of the afternoon. Ki began to climb in his easy, almost effortless way. He leaped to a huge boulder and, just as he was pulling himself over its crown, he heard an ominious rattle. Ki froze for an instant to see a six-foot-long diamondback rattlesnake only inches from where his hand was resting. The reptile was coiled, waiting for some prehistoric message to touch its killing brain and order it to strike.

Ki tensed. His years of training told him that he was faster than the head of the serpent, but he had never tested the theory and he did not wish to taste the poisonous venom. Still, he had to move, and so he prepared his free hand to grab. The rattler's small black eyes were fixed on its target and when it struck, Ki's free hand was a blur as he grabbed the serpent just below its hinged jaws. An instant later, his *tanto* blade flashed and the rattler's ugly head, jaws still opening and closing spasmodically, dropped to empty itself of blood on the warm rocks. Ki hefted the thick, wriggling weight of the diamondback. The snake would be good eating; its heavy muscle outweighed that of any two rabbits he had killed.

From his new vantage point atop the rocks, Ki could see in all directions for many miles. But his eyes moved to the catch corral, and he searched for activity. For almost a full minute, he saw nothing, and then he stiffened when he noticed Pete's legs protruding from the brush, toes down. Something told Ki that the old mustanger was dead.

A sudden movement caught his attention. Ki's keen eyes moved a fraction of an inch and now he saw Bloody Knife. The Shoshone swung the heavy corral gate open, then dashed into the corral, where he began to wave a blanket at the mustangs. He was turning them all loose!

Ki began to jump from rock to rock. He bounded like a panther from the rock shelf and then leapt into the sage. But he was too late. Much too late. The mustangs were already scattering into the desert.

Ki ran with an economy of motion that was silken smooth and utterly graceful. His lithe body traveled with deceptive speed and his breathing hardly quickened at all. When he neared the corral, the dust was so thick it obscured his view of the area around the camp.

The thick dust was the only thing that gave the Indian enough of an advantage to take aim with his rifle and send a bullet into Ki's side. Ki twisted with the impact of the lead ball, his body seeming to lose its strength just as the air would suddenly explode out of a punctured balloon. His legs buckled and the bow and arrow he had nocked slipped from his hand as he fell, clutching his side.

Ki rolled over and over, staying low in the sagebrush. His fingers probed the lining of his vest and found one of the star-blade *shuriken*. He waited with grim patience for Bloody Knife to finish his kill.

The minutes dragged on slowly. Ki could feel his heart pumping blood that pulsed at his wet fingertips. He stayed pressed to the ground and poked a finger into the bullet hole just below his ribs to stop the bleeding.

Then he heard the galloping hooves of a lone horse as it departed the camp, echoing into the distance. Ki pushed himself to his knees, then found the strength to rise to his feet. He stood swaying, watching the Indian disappear into the fading sunset. A cold light gleamed in his black eyes and he found the strength to pick up his bow and arrow. His fingertip had stanched the flow of blood and he knew that the bullet rested deep in a layer of muscle. Bloody Knife's weapon had fired its bullet true, but the Indian had tried to save gunpowder and had not set a sufficient charge to kill a strong man.

"I am coming for you," Ki said between gritted teeth. "And I will show no mercy."

They found him staggering through his pain and the darkness of night, more dead than alive. The blood of the rabbits, sage hen, and rattlesnake had mixed with his own to cover the lower half of his pants.

Despite their protests, Ki shunned any support. He moved to the campfire and stared across the flames at Bloody Knife, who crouched like a cornered animal. The Indian wore a mixed expression of hatred and astonishment. There was something in Ki's stance and appearance that chilled even the outcast Shoshone's heart when he looked at the man he thought must surely have died.

Ki's voice was steady, but he breathed very deep and slow. "You killed our friend Pete and set the mustangs free. Why?"

Bloody Knife managed to rise to his full height. He argued in a flat, guttural voice to the Indians who stared at him. His words were like a lash that whipped at the tribe, and Three Kills roared back at him.

Suddenly, Bloody Knife's jaw dropped and his arrogance was gone. He stared around the circle of accusing faces.

Three Kills said, "He denied what Ki accused him of, even though he did not know his language. It proved his guilt."

The Indian chief's hand moved toward his knife and the Shoshone whirled to run. Ki's bow bent with the last of his strength, and when the arrow left his bowstring it sang its name, which in English meant "death's song." In place of an arrowhead, the arrow had a small ceramic bulb with a hole in it, and the air whistled as the arrow pierced the night with a very high, keening sound, ending in a fleshy thud. Bloody Knife's arms and shoulders were wrenched backward like the wings of a trapped bird. His chest protruded and the "death's song" arrow escaped his body just below the rib cage.

The Indian took two faltering steps and pitched forward, dead before his face struck the ground.

Ki's legs buckled and he was ashamed as he began to sag. Jessie and Mark caught him before he collapsed.

"Bring him into my house," Three Kills ordered quickly. "Chena knows some medicine."

"So do I," Jessie said, her voice stretched thin to the point of breaking. "I've dug more than one bullet out of a good man. But none better than Ki. Ask someone to boil water, quickly!"

Ki felt himself being lowered to a soft mat of branches covered with blankets. He wanted to sleep, but knew that he could not.

"Jessie," he whispered.

"I'm right here."

"Do not be afraid to cut deep and clean. Remember, I am one who has prepared himself for *seppuku*, with two swift cuts to—"

"Be quiet," Jessie said, sniffling and roughly wiping away a flood of tears with the back of her sleeve. "If you ever try to disembowel yourself like those dumb old ancestors on your mother's side, I'll kill you myself!"

Ki smiled weakly. "It's good to know that when you are very upset, even you do not not make sense, Jessie." He reached down and gave her his *tanto* blade and said, "Cut deep and clean, and I promise you I will not die."

She bit her lip until she tasted blood. "You'd better not," she warned. "Without you at my side, the Starbuck empire would be in a terrible fix. My own life would be in grave jeopardy after all the enemies we have made together."

This time Kid did not smile, because he knew what she said was true. Jessie was strong, stronger than any woman he had ever met. She feared nothing and would die giving her own life to save his. That was why he was so devoted to life, because she needed him to shield her from a host of jealous and ruthless enemies.

Ki watched as Jessie bent forward with the razor-sharp blade. "Even if you commit a butchery," he confided to her with a wink, "I will still live."

"Why didn't you tell me that a samurai's skin could be pierced with a bullet?" she demanded with mock anger.

Ki started to answer, but then the blade drove into his flesh and he discovered that even one trained as a samurai could not talk and be operated upon at the same moment in time.

# Chapter 7

They had found Pete's body in the brush beside the buckboard. He had been cutting firewood and Bloody Knife had managed to sneak up from behind and drive a blade deep into his back.

Ki, though extremely weak, had wanted to come to the burying, but Jessie had insisted he remain in Three Kills' lodge. He had lost too much blood already and he needed to remain stationary long enough to allow his bullet wound to heal properly. He had gone through an ordeal that would have killed most men and Jessie did not want to take any more chances with his life.

Early the very next morning they buried Pete on a knoll overlooking his catch corral. Jessie did not have a Bible, so she said the words of the Twenty-third Psalm by heart over Pete's grave. It was only as they were leaving to go mustanging that Jessie realized she had never even learned Pete's last name or if he had any family she needed to write. *I know nothing of him, really. Only that he loved horses, was afraid of Indians, and that we talked him into coming down here, which cost the man his life.*

Chief Three Kills and the people of his camp also seemed troubled and saddened by the death of the mustanger. Pete had posed no threat to anyone. He had only wanted to be left alone and in peace. His death by Bloody Knife brought shame upon these Indians, because it was a brutal and unnecessary murder.

With the burying finished, Jessie knew that it was time to start catching wild horses. She had enough men now, and Pete had told her dozens of stories about his mustanging.

"We'll start with the bands that Bloody Knife turned loose," she said. "Follow their tracks and round them up again. We'll need every wild horse on this range. As soon as we've cleared it of mustangs, we'll have to disassemble the corral and haul it to a new site and start all over."

Mark agreed, and so the hunt began anew. It was with a sad and empty feeling that they rode into the hills, missing Pete's happy, constant reminiscing of mustang stories. But they went, and Jessie tried to recall everything she had learned from the Elko mustanger that would help her make this first day's hunt a success.

She divided their forces. Mark took a small group of mustangers to the west, Three Kills led four of his best men east, and Jessie took the rest of the Indians and went after the chestnut stallion and his large band that Bloody Knife had turned loose.

The trail of the chestnut and his mares was easy to follow and they had no trouble locating the band by late afternoon. Without needing to give anything more than a very few hand signals, Jessie indicated to the Indians that a few of their number should circle the band while the others should post themselves in two parallel lines, forming a gauntlet through which the mustangs would have to run.

Jessie waited while the Indians took their places. Her eyes surveyed every contour of the land between herself and the catch corral. Her mind registered each spot between here and the corral where the chestnut would see an escape route. This time the task of driving that stallion into the catch corral would be even more difficult.

Jessie untied her lariat, wishing she were mounted on her own magnificent palomino stallion, Sun, which she had left in Texas when she went to the cattlemen's convention. *If I had known I would be spending so much time in the saddle*, she thought, *I would have had Sun shipped out here by rail*.

The horse underneath her quivered with excitement. It was a roan gelding, long-legged and deep of chest. Jessie knew the horse was superior to any of the mustang mares she would soon be chasing but, carrying her weight and that of the saddle, it was no match for the chestnut stallion beyond the distance of a few miles.

*I must be the closest to the corral,* she decided, urging the roan back in the direction of her camp. *And when the chestnut stallion tries to break, I'll be the only one who has a chance of stopping him*.

The Indians came boiling into her sight with the chestnut and his band of horses running before them. Jessie pulled her roan into an outcropping of rocks and dismounted, then climbed to a higher vantage point.

"Yes!" she whispered, seeing the Indians begin to squeeze the racing mustangs and keep them running bunched in the right direction. "Don't let them turn!"

She needn't have worried. The Indians knew what they were doing. Each time the stallion tried to lead his mares either to the right or the left, one of Three Kills' men seemed to appear from nowhere and cut off the attempt.

And now, as the mustangs swept closer, Jessie dashed back to her gelding and timed her entrance into the roundup perfectly. The chestnut had been waiting to break away and now the land favored his intentions, with a sharp draw veering off to the south. Jessie anticipated his move and drove her spurs into the gelding, and the animal swept into the path of the stallion.

"Ya!" she cried, swinging her lariat. The stallion hesitated for an instant and Jessie made her toss. The loop flew to its mark, and settled neatly over the stallion's head. She dallied the rope and when the animal tried to knock her racing mount over, Jessie lashed it across the face with a quirt. The animal gave up and ran with its ears back.

The rest was easy. They allowed the mares to slow enough not to wind themselves too badly and, easy as could be, they finished the roundup without further mishap.

By the end of that first day, when Mark and Three Kills had caught their bands, the tally of mustangs stood at one hundred and forty-six horses. There were smiles on the Indians' faces, at least partly, Jessie knew, because of the money she had promised to pay them for catching these wild horses. At ten dollars a head, this poverty-ridden tribe would make almost fifteen hundred dollars from today's work, and that was enough to buy food and clothing to last them an entire year. Tomorrow, the money they earned would begin to add up toward ownership of land.

"At this rate," Mark said proudly as he surveyed the mustangs, "we'd be out of here by the end of August."

"But it won't be like this every day," Jessie told him. It was a warm, star-studded evening. Everyone was tired but feeling good about the way the first day had turned out so successfully.

Jessie laid her cheek on the top rail of the corral and turned to look at Mark. "I'd say from the tracks and signs out there, we have another five or six days in this country before we sweep it clean. After that, we'll have to take down the corrals and move them at least twenty or thirty miles."

"And what will we do with the mustangs that we have already caught?"

"I'm not sure," she confessed. "There is just not enough feed out here to hold four or five hundred horses in one place more than a day or two. I'd say that we'll have to take them to Elko in batches and ship them to Denver for safekeeping."

"But what about the revolutionaries? If they catch word of our plan, there will be no one in Denver to stop them from just stealing the mustangs we send."

"Not so," Jessie replied. "We've both crews on a payroll, haven't we?"

"Yes, but . . ."

Jessie immediately understood Mark's hesitation and wished she could take back her last words. It wasn't that Mark was any less committed to this mustanging business than she, but only that he lacked the resources she could call on in a time of great need. The Starbuck empire was vast and hugely profitable. In times like these when cattle prices were low, she simply relied more on the revenue gained from one of her many other ventures. Mark and his father were not big enough to have the luxury of diversification, and that was why he was dubious his father could spare the men or money to send to Denver.

"Mark, listen to me," she said, wanting to make him know her feelings. "You'll have to understand that sometimes I forget that I run an empire, and that I have all the men and money I need in a crisis like this."

"I know that," he said. "You'd never boast or let on for a minute what you are worth, Jessie. It's just that . . . well, being around a woman as rich and powerful—and downright beautiful—as you can be a little unnerving sometimes. Makes a man feel that he has nothing to offer."

A knowing smile touched Jessie's full lips. She understood perfectly, because many men felt that way about her. "The kind of man that attracts me might own a ranch, or nothing but a horse, rifle, and the clothes he wears," she said evenly. "Money has nothing to do with my feelings about strong men. You are strong, Mark. I knew that when you defied your peers in Denver and stood up for what you believed, and fought beside Ki and me against the opposition."

"You would have done fine without my help."

"Not so. If it wasn't for you, I wouldn't have gotten involved in this, and the history of Mexico might be the worse for it. I need Ki, but I also need you, Mark."

He took a deep breath and pulled her close. His lips sought hers and their tongues met. Jessie felt the heat rise up through her aching loins.

"Come on," she said. "If you're ready for a real ride, come with me."

He nodded, dry-mouthed and realizing that, at last, they would make love. The weariness of a long, long day fell from his body and he hurried after Jessica Starbuck, following her swaying hips into the sage and the sweet, sage-scented night.

Ki chafed at not being fit enough to ride a galloping horse and join the mustangers. He was a restless man, one not comfortable being idle when others were spending twelve or fourteen hours in the saddle. Each day of this past week he had been rising at dawn. Chena had risen too, and she insisted they needed to walk farther and farther into the desert mountains to build up his strength and endurance. On this fine morning they had reached a high place almost ten miles from camp.

The day was warm, the air still and unmoving. Ki sat on the rock cross-legged and closed his eyes to better taste and feel the earth, and a sun that was still climbing out of the eastern horizon. It was good to be alive. Chena sat close beside him and he considered again the fact that she was very attracted to him. She was a strikingly handsome young woman, generous of lips and breasts. He wondered what would happen to her after the mustanging. Ki hoped that her father would allow her to stay rather then be sent off to the white man's cities.

"What are you thinking about, Ki?" she asked, almost afraid to disturb his thoughts.

Ki knew what she wanted to hear and it was easy to tell her the truth. "My thoughts were of you and the welfare of your people."

"But mostly of me?" she pressed eagerly.

"Yes."

"And not of Miss Starbuck?"

"Not now."

"But you love her, don't you." It was not a question, but a statement of fact.

"Yes," he admitted. "But not in the way of most men and women. Our bodies will never be one. I have sworn upon my honor to help and protect her. I will always do that."

"But why?"

Chena pushed up against him and he could feel the heat of her body as she reached out to touch the smooth, flat muscles of his chest. "Ki, I do not understand. You are a man and yet you say you do not lie with her. A man needs to lie with a woman sometimes. Don't you?"

There was the faintest edge of concern in her voice, and it made Ki smile, because other women had also voiced that same alarm when he admitted that he and Jessie were not lovers.

"I am normal, Chena. If it helps you to understand, think of Jessie and me as brother and sister. There is love, but not a joining of the flesh."

Chena relaxed and smiled. "I see now. Yes. That is good."

Surer of her success, Chena's hands moved lower on his chest until she touched the bandaged place where he had been shot, the place where Jessie had placed the tip of the *tanto* knife and fished out the lead ball from deep inside.

"Ki, if we . . . would it . . . ?"

"No," he said, guessing her meaning. "It would not hurt me inside, but it might you."

She looked him squarely in the eye. "I have had a

man before." When his eyes probed hers, seeking the truth, Chena looked away and added shyly, "Almost."

He laughed. "What does that mean?"

She became embarrassed and looked downward. "There was a boy. His name was Little Elk and he and I were in love. Bloody Knife caught us alone in the grass one day. The boy was still small and not all the way inside me yet when Bloody Knife yanked him off and beat him. Bloody Knife took me to my father and said that he wanted me as his wife. I refused. And that has been the way of it since then."

"And the boy?" Ki asked. "What became of him?"

"He grew to be a man, but he would never look at me again. Last winter, when it snowed for so long and the children were starving, Little Elk went out to hunt in a blizzard. I saw him. I told him to stop, that he would find nothing in a blizzard."

Chena took a deep, shuddering breath. "I was wrong. He found the white death."

Her eyes were glistening and Ki knew how much the pain of losing that man must have hurt. Ki wrapped his arms around the halfbreed girl, wishing he could somehow erase her pain. But that was impossible. Pain and the loss of loved ones were part of life and he had known more than his own share.

"Ki, love me now," she pleaded, pushing back his vest and kissing his chest. She took one of his nipples in her lips and sucked on it until he felt his manhood begin to awaken. This was a virgin girl, however, and a man could never forgive himself by hurting such a person dishonorably. "Maybe there will be another Little Elk and you should wait."

"No," she said, gently pushing him back on the warm rock. "He is gone and I will never be a girl again. And yet, I am not quite a woman, either. Don't you see my need? I thought you would understand. We are both halfbreed people, Ki. We have a special understanding between us."

He swallowed noisily, felt the blood begin to pound faster in his veins. Her mouth found his and her lips fired his passion. Ki rolled her sideways until she was lying flat on the rock. He began to undress the halfbreed girl and when she lay before him naked and unashamed, he smiled with admiration.

"You are beautiful, Chena," he said softly, and she smiled, knowing it was true. Her breasts were larger than he had expected, full and firm, with large, dark nipples. When his tongue darted out to lave them, they stood proud.

She moaned with soft delight and his fingers moved down to touch the crescent-shaped union of her womanhood. She was slender in the waist, her hips flaring sensuously into legs that were long and perfectly formed.

Her eyes were open as she watched him, and when Ki touched the secret places deep in the mass of silken hair between her legs, she was already wet and filled with a woman's juices. Her lips parted and she began to breathe quickly.

Ki pulled away from her and she grabbed for him, but he smiled. "I think I had better take my pants off, Chena, and let you make sure you know what you are getting."

She nodded mutely. There was a line of perspiration on her upper lip and she licked it off as she stared at his crotch. Chena watched him with both hunger and fascination as he untied the sash at his waist and slipped out of his black pants. When his manhood sprung free from the constriction of his clothing, she gasped with shock and amazement.

"Ki," she whispered, staring at his immense, throbbing member, "I did not know men could be like that. Little Elk—"

He knelt beside her. "Little Elk was a boy and you were curious children. You're no child anymore. Chena."

He reached out and slipped his finger into her wetness, and she arched her back and groaned. But it was a sound of pleasure and not of pain, and Ki was at last fully satisfied that this virgin halfbreed girl was ready for a man. It had been a long, long time since he had made love to a virgin, and he felt it an honor and a privilege. He would do so in a way that would be gentle, but one that would show her how a man and a woman could bring great pleasure to each other. Ki was a man who prided himself on making a woman achieve ecstasy.

As his finger slipped in and out of Chena's hot slickness, an almost glazed expression of pleasure filmed her lovely eyes. Her hips begin to rock back and forth and she took his wrist and pushed his finger in deeper and deeper until she was gasping and writhing.

"Oh, Ki, I think I want you now!"

"I think you do too," he said, easing her back on the rock again. "Take me, Chena. Hold me in your hand and then you put me inside of you slowly. If it hurts, stop for a moment, and the pain will ease and become pleasure again."

She nodded, cradling his manhood in both hands as if it were a rare treasure. Chena took a resolute breath, then spread her legs out very wide on the rock and pressed the head of his member to her soft and eager womanhood. When he rocked his hips forward a little, he felt the heat of her close hungrily around him. The woman scent of her desire was strong and it fed his hunger, making it almost impossible not to thrust deeply.

Her chest was heaving and he could feel her heart race. Ki slid into her another inch and she was as hot as a fire. Her eyes rolled upward and suddenly she released his manhood to grab his muscled buttocks.

"Oh . . . oh, now!" she screamed. "Deep in me now!"

Ki rocked his hips forward, feeling his staff drive

into her hot depths. Chena reacted by yelping with an ecstasy that filled the air and echoed through the rocky hills. Her long legs thrashed and her heels began to beat against the rock.

Ki tried to pull back for a minute to make it last longer for her, but she locked her legs around the small of his back. He was powerless to break free as she lost control of her body and bucked wildly to a shuddering climax.

Chena's heart was beating so rapidly Ki could see a pulse beating at the base of her throat. Her eyes were closed and for a moment Ki feared she might have lost consciousness.

"Chena!" he whispered urgently.

Her eyes fluttered open and she smiled, tigerlike. "I am not finished, am I?"

He grinned and shoved himself all the way back inside her. His hips began to move in a slow ellipse that would quickly restore her need to match his own. "No," he said to her, "you are only beginning."

"Oh, I hope so! I . . . oh, Ki," she choked as her body began to thrust as if it were a thing separate and completely uncontrollable. "I never knew it could be like this."

There are times when words are superfluous and this was definitely one of them. Ki began to thrust harder and deeper. His strokes grew more and more frenzied. Chena was moaning and screaming again so loudly that it sounded like she was dying of joy. He would have to teach her to be more silent, for they would not always have the entire desert for her to serenade.

But he would teach her that later in the day. For right now, he would let her scream like a wildcat. Faster and faster their bodies drove at each other, until finally they were both out of control and Ki was quenching both of their fires with great, drenching bursts of his seed.

# Chapter 8

Ki and Chena sat deep within the small hole and waited for the mustangs to come to drink again. It was very late afternoon and they had been crouched unmoving for nearly four hours, but Ki knew the mustangs were coming; the day had been hot and they would be very thirsty.

Ki intended to catch a fine sorrel stallion that Chena had seen one afternoon and fallen in love with. The young stallion also had a small but nice band of mares, which would bring the total number of mustangs caught so far up to almost five hundred. Tomorrow they would be moving the catch corral and leaving this territory for fresh mustanging country, so Ki had decided to use a foot trap and do this for Chena.

The halfbreed girl touched his cheek and whispered, "Are you sure you remember what Pete told you to do if we catch the stallion?"

"Yes," Ki deadpanned. "He said to hang on tight."

Chena giggled like a schoolgirl and touched him with intimacy. "I wish this hole were bigger so we could enjoy our stay here together."

"Well, it's not, so we must be—" He stopped, pressed his ear to their earthen wall, and listened intently. Satisfied, he nodded and whispered, "They come!"

The foot trap that Ki was counting on was a very simple device. It consisted of nothing but a loop supported by a thin layer of twigs and covered with a layer of dirt. The stallion would step through the loop and the snapping twigs would signal the proper moment to yank the buried rope that led to Ki's hands. If all went as planned, they would have a wild mustang by the fore-foot and it would be about like holding an alligator by the tail. Pete had advised that a mustanger ought to tie the rope to a log that could be dragged far enough to tire the stallion. Ki had rejected that idea. Tied to a log, the rope would saw at a fighting stallion's leg and might accidentally injure or even break it. Ki did not intend to take the chance of that happening. He figured he would test his own growing strength against that of the stallion. If he won, not only would he have a sound horse to give Chena, but he'd also have proven to himself that he was fully healed.

They sensed the horses as they approached the water hole along a narrow, twisting path through the sage. It was a path that mustangs had been following for years, and which was now cut quite deeply into the pale, soft earth. Chena tensed and Ki felt her grip on his arm tighten. He could taste dust lifted by the stallion's hooves.

The twigs snapped like tiny bones. Ki jerked on the rope and heard the stallion trumpet in alarm as his mares scattered. The rope yanked Ki upward so powerfully that he became airborne. He was dragged and when the stallion whirled on him its eyes shone like rare topaz. Ki lunged to his feet and threw his weight behind the rope. The stallion crashed to the earth. Ki started to jump for its back but the enraged animal snapped at him with its teeth. Ki retreated for a moment and the horse was back up and fighting the rope.

Chena tried to grab it but Ki shouted, "No, stay back until I subdue him!"

"But how?"

The stallion reared again and almost stomped them

both. Ki pushed Chena back into the protection of the hole and removed a lariat he had tied around his waist. The animal lunged at Ki and he dodged out of its path, still holding onto the rope from the foot trap.

Ki dug his heels in and pulled the stallion around. When it reared once more, he swung the lariat overhead three times and let it fly over the stallion's head. He tightened it as it settled around the enraged animal's legs, binding them together tightly. The sorrel crashed to the dirt, toppling heavily.

"You can come out now," Ki said, reaching out and helping Chena back up to ground level. "We had better go after his mares, though I doubt they'll scatter very far without their leader."

Chena looked from the thrashing but obviously immobilized stallion to Ki. "Yes!" she laughed. "Let us catch the mares, for it is clear this stallion is helpless."

And that is just what they did.


Jessie studied the huge corralful of mustangs.

She and Ki, along with Mark and Three Kills, had talked things over very carefully. It was the end of August and the springs were running low. The available grass was burnt and strawlike with little nourishment. They simply could not keep the captured mustangs any longer or they would starve. It had been decided that she and Ki, along with five of the Indians, would herd this first half of the necessary mustangs to Elko. There, she would have the mustangs freighted to Denver, where her experienced Circle Star cowboys would meet and hold them. With luck, by the time she and Ki returned, another hundred wild horses would have been captured, and they could finish mustanging by the end of September. After that, all that would be necessary would be to board the train with the new horses, gather those in Denver, and push on down to the Mexican border. Arrangements could easily be made to deliver the badly needed horses to President González's army representatives. It sounded very simple, but Jessie knew that even simple plans had a way of going awry.

"Now," Ki said skeptically to her, "all we have to do is figure out how you and I and a handful of Indians are going to control and drive five hundred wild horses. I don't see how we can rope them all together."

"We don't," Jessie said, a little bit proud of herself because she alone had thought to once ask Pete how mustangs were controlled after capture. She had learned the answer in great and almost painful detail.

"A lot of mustangers blindfold 'em, then wire up their nostrils so they can't breathe well enough to run."

"I'd never do that!" Jessie had said angrily. "And if I saw it done, there'd be hell to pay."

"Don't blame ya," Pete had drawled. "Some other mustangers, knowing that their horses are just going to the slaughterhouses, they cut the knee joint and drain the joint water so the mustang can't bend his leg without pain."

"That's even worse!" Jessie had shaken her tawny mane with anger. "Surely there is an effective and relatively painless way to get captured mustangs from one place to another."

"There is," Pete said, "and it's the one we'll use, all right."

He had gone on to explain how a single man could control a hundred wild mustangs without using any drastically cruel methods. All he had to do was tie the mustang's head to his tail and "bend him just enough so that if he tried to run, he'll go around and around in small circles."

Jessie had applauded the trick with enthusiasm, for it was simple and painless, but would obviously be extremely effective. No horse alive could run with its head bent toward its tail.

They spent an entire day tying heads to tails and left

for Elko at once. Three Kills' Indians would not go all the way into town, but would return as soon as the town was in sight.

One week later, the tall and strikingly handsome young man who had waited impatiently for over a month just south of Elko peered through a seaman's telescope. *"Bueno,"* he grated to himself. "It's about time you got here! Armando Escobar needs those horses, Señorita Starbuck!"

Toro Montoya grinned, his mouth generous, all his teeth amazingly white and even. He was dark-complexioned, and yet his nose was sharp and slightly bent outward, unlike that of most Mexicans or Indians. His speech and dress were refined and proclaimed him to be a person of some wealth and importance. A stranger might have studied his hard but noble face and guessed him to be the son of a wealthy ranch owner. They would have been incorrect, for Toro was raised to be a bullfighter in Spain. His Spanish ancestors had always been bullfighters and he would have been too, had it not been for the fact that he had been foolish enough to seduce a matador's woman, and then been forced to kill the enraged national hero. They had fought with estoques, the long blades used to determine the bull's courage at the moment of its death. Toro had played the enraged Ortiz like a bull, and killed him just as expertly as he would have a bull, using a thrust to the shoulder that went deep and severed the aorta in an almost bloodless kill. For this, Toro had barely escaped into Portugal with his young life as thousands of Spaniards set up a hue and cry for his head.

For a time, Toro had hidden, but the lust for the bullring had drawn him like the scent of a woman in readiness for love. He had found life unbearable without the bulls and had fought in small bullrings under many names until his grace, courage, and skill had quickly attracted large, adoring crowds—and avenging Spaniards, who would never forgive him for killing their national hero, José Ortiz. Finally, Toro had fled to Mexico, where he had met Armando Escobar, leader of a new revolution, aficionado of the ring. A deal had been struck—help Escobar topple the government of Presidente Manuel González, and the great arena in Mexico City would become Toro's world stage.

Toro had accepted. He would have offered to do anything to have the chance to be a bullfighter once more. It was, quite simply, all that he had ever wanted, the thing for which he had been born.

He replaced the telescope in its leather case and moved back to his camp hidden among a stand of trees. Toro smiled wolfishly, for he had not only seen the mustangs so badly needed by the revolutionaries, but he had also studied the rich American *señorita*. Jessica Starbuck was even more beautiful than he had been told she would be. Toro was not a man to force himself upon any woman. He had been raised the son of a noble Spaniard and women were inviolate—if they insisted. But there had never been a woman that he had not been able to seduce, especially one who saw him fight the bulls.

He shook his head. "The mustangs first, the woman second, Toro. Once you deliver the mustangs and become the most famous matador of Mexico, you can have every woman you desire. Your orders are to get the horses without creating any trouble with the American government. To become that woman's lover might create many unnecessary problems. Get the horses first, Toro. Later, you can invite her to watch you kill the bulls and she will beg you to make love to her!"

Toro laughed out loud. The sound of it carried to the trees and his men fell silent, for Toro had been in a savage temper for weeks. A man of his temperament was not used to waiting and preferred action to inaction.

The men around the camp smiled. Without even hearing their leader say it, they knew that the waiting was over.

"What do we do now?" a man asked when he told them about the approaching mustangs being driven by Jessica, Ki, and a small band of Indians.

Toro twisted the ends of his long mustache, which was waxed like the tips of the bull's horns. "We do nothing," he said, knowing that he had to be patient a little while longer. "We wait and see what they do first."

"We're getting paid the same, ain't we?" a thick-necked and coarse man demanded.

Toro scowled. He had not dared to bring a collection of Mexican revolutionaries across the border, for they would have been too obvious and caused alarm and questions. Instead, he had been forced to hire a band of gringo gunmen, none of whom he trusted or liked. They knew nothing of bullfighting, so they were obviously uncultured and beneath his station of dignity. Toro had disdainfully concluded that these killers were little more than American *peones*. But they were deadly, and while a matador was brave, he was also never foolish or stupid. Toro tolerated these men because he had no choice.

"Well, ain't we gettin' paid the same?"

"Of course. You are getting paid by the man who pays me, Armando Escobar. You have already been paid something, the rest is waiting when we have all the horses."

The man rumbled like a cow in labor. His name was Paul, and he was the strongest, though Toro suspected also the stupidest. There were others that he knew to be more dangerous. Men who killed with a smile, like that of a matador when he played with the bull and sank the picadors.

Their cold, pale eyes watched and measured him with calculation. "Come," he said in flawless English but feeling a rivulet of sweat trickle down his spine, "let's watch them and see where they take the wild horses."

"Why don't we hit 'em now?" Paul grumbled. "We could kill 'em all and bury 'em so nobody would ever know they caught those mustangs."

Toro was tempted to agree that the the suggestion had merit. But the idea of killing a beautiful woman was repugnant and, besides, Miss Starbuck was so famous that her absence would immediately raise a flood of unwelcome attention. Much better, Toro decided, if he could just steal the horses and perhaps even the beautiful *señorita*'s favors. As for Mark Lyon, well, his death would leave no sorrow in any heart except that of his father. Toro had been in the back of the convention hall when Jessica Starbuck had given her speech at the cattlemen's meeting. He had seen Mark Lyon fight for the woman's honor and had not been unduly impressed with the son of the New Mexico rancher. The man who had impressed Toro was Ki, a strange and deadly mixture of Caucasian and Oriental, possessing the best features of both races. The man was graceful enough even to be a matador! Toro had made it his business to learn more about Ki, and what he had discovered made him very cautious indeed.

He looked at his men. "Because the rancher's son, the one called Mark, is not with them now but remains on the range, I think they will catch more mustangs before the summer is over," he said slowly, making his decision as he spoke. "If that is true, then it would be foolish to kill them now. We wait and watch. We let them to do the work and when the time is perfect, we strike!"

Paul looked disappointed but shrugged his big, sloping shoulders and ambled away. "Long as we get paid the same, I'll stay here and sleep until the goddamn snow falls or the food runs out," he grumbled.

Toro scowled. He ordered his men to keep well hidden in the trees and then he saddled his horse and waited for the mustangers to pass on their return to Elko.

\* \* \*

Three miles outside of town, Jessie indicated that the Indians had come far enough, and they turned back with obvious relief. The mustangs were weary and understood very well that any attempt to run would be futile. She and Ki had no trouble whatsoever bringing them in the rest of the way to the railroad stockyards. They found a pair of empty corrals large enough to hold the mustangs and quickly moved toward the railroad office.

"I want these five hundred head of mustangs shipped out on the first train to Denver," she instructed.

"I'm sorry, ma'am," the Central Pacific railroad-office manager replied. "Every stockcar rolling east for the next month and a half is taken. Cattlemen in these parts are selling for whatever they can get for their cattle before they wither up and die of hunger or thirst."

Jessie scowled. "All right," she said finally, "I'll buy the next shipment of cattle to be loaded from here for whatever price the seller received back east."

"But you wouldn't have to pay that much, because the seller is figuring in shipping costs."

"So am I," Jessie said. "Ship the cattle to the Circle Star ranch in care of my foreman, Ed Wright."

"Yes, ma'am!"

Jessie smiled. "I'll also need hay and grain for the mustangs and a veterinarian to check them over for soundness."·

"Feed is awful expensive right now, Miss . . . ?"

Jessie did not want her real name to come out and be gobbled up by the newspaper. "I'll pay whatever it costs," she said, silencing the railroad man's inquiry. "Just get it done and I'll bring the money in the morning."

"Consider it taken care of," he said officiously. "I am a man who gets things done."

"I can count on that?"

"You bet," he said with a short nod of his head.

"Good," Jessie said. "You are a rare man and ought

to be commended." It was not idle flattery. Whenever she met a man more concerned with results than rules, regulations, and his retirement, Jessie was impressed.

She and Ki left at once and headed for the telegraph office. Inside, she was given a form and told that the lines were tied up but that her message would be sent within the next hour.

Jessie smiled wearily. She wanted a bath and a bed, in that order. "That will be plenty soon enough," she told the telegraph operator as she scribbled out her message to her trusted foreman, Ed Wright. The message ordered him to immediately send a crew of ten men to Denver to meet and guard the mustangs until further notice. She told him that she would telegraph again to let him know when she and Ki would accompany a second shipment of five hundred mustangs.

"Long message, miss," he said, counting every word twice. "I'm afraid it's going to cost seven dollars and thirty-five cents. Sorry."

"That's all right," Jessie said, pulling out a second message that Mark had sent telling his father little more than that he was fine and everything was going as planned.

"This one will just cost three dollars," the telegraph operator said, looking happy that the charge was lower.

Jessie paid the man and left. The telegraph operator went back to work after neatly stacking both messages in a wire basket placed on his wooden counter.

Toro Montoya waited until Jessie and Ki entered the hotel and then he moved quickly toward the telegraph office. He had already guessed Jessie's conversation with the Central Pacific man and did not need to squeeze from him any information. Now, as he entered the telegraph office, his lean, handsome face assumed an air of pleasant confidence.

"Yes, sir," the operator said, "how can I help you?"

"I want to send a telegraph," Toro decided, his eyes

coming to rest on the wire basket. He tried to avoid staring at Jessie's message. "Right away, please."

"Where to, sir?"

"Juárez, Mexico." There was a magnificent *señorita* that he wanted to see again when this business was finished.

"I'm sorry, but this company doesn't send messages across the border. We will someday, but—"

"Never mind. I will send one to . . . to Denver."

He was given the form and scribbled a short message to a fictitious person that read:

ALL IS WELL STOP WILL ARRIVE SOON STOP MISS YOU STOP

The clerk read it, counting the words.

"Might be an hour or so."

"That's fine. The wife hasn't heard from me in two weeks, another few minutes won't matter."

"Sure. I understand. Have a wife and kids myself and I once took a trip to St. Louis. I sent—"

"How much do I owe you?" Toro interrupted softly.

The telegraph operator was caught with his mouth flapping. He clamped it shut. The smile on his chubby face evaporated and he became quite businesslike. "One dollar. Minimum charge here."

Toro paid and watched the man drop the message into the wire basket. He waited until the operator turned, then he deftly lifted Jessie's message. He noticed the one from Mark Lyon to his father in New Mexico and lifted that one too, slipping them both into his vest pocket.

"Thanks!" he called to the man, who was now scribbling out a message that was coming in on the lines. The operator did not even hear him and Toro left the office with a large smile on his aristocratic face. He could whistle like a whippoorwill and play flamenco

102

music on a guitar so beautifully it made *señoritas* weep and filled their hearts with love. Now, as he strode down the boardwalk with a tune on his lips and a smile on his face, he was followed by the admiring eyes of every woman who saw him. Toro Montoya, the famous matador and slayer of bulls and ladies—could any man seek to achieve more in this world?

When he returned to his camp, he grew serious. Too long he had been trapped with these primitive men and had hungered for the charms of ladies.

"We are leaving on the train," he told his men. "We are taking the mustangs to Denver."

"Without a fight?"

Toro thought of the telegrams crumpled up in his pocket. He removed them, then pitched them into the campfire. "Yes." He grinned. "Without a fight—this time."

Paul looked disappointed but the others smiled, because Toro had the kind of grin that was mischievous and infectious. They were leaving for Denver, and still on the payroll of Armando Escobar and the Mexican revolutionaries.

# Chapter 9

When Jessie awoke one morning to find ice encrusted around the edges of the creek, she realized that September had swept past and it was turning autumn. Her green eyes lifted toward the cottonwood trees that followed the precious water throughout this rugged country. The leaves were turning gold, crimson, and orange. *My God,* she thought, *where has the summer gone?*

This had been one of the hardest and yet most satisfying times of her life. She had caught mustang fever with all its danger and excitement. The three hundred mustangs they now held, in addition to those she had sent on to Denver, brought the total to eight hundred. Both she and Ki knew that the Circle Star could provide the rest, but catching a thousand mustangs had become an obsession. Besides, these Nevada mustangs were terribly thin, and Jessie felt they could not help but fare better as Mexican army mounts. Down in Mexico, where men traveled primarily on foot, a good saddle horse was a luxury and a sign of importance. A man might allow his wife and children to go hungry now and then, but not his saddle horse.

They had moved the huge catch corral hoping this final location would net them the remaining mustangs. By now, they were all quite expert mustangers, at least compared to how they had started. Rarely did they fail to catch every wild band of horses that moved within a thirty-mile circumference of their catch corral.

They had been driving themselves at a killing pace. They were in the saddle long before daylight and never left it until after sunset. Mark finally decided they needed to saddle-break a few mustangs because they were wearing out their own saddle horses and needed fresh replacements.

"If we keep riding our horses any longer," he said, "we'll kill them. They're stumbling with weariness and someone else is going to get piled."

Jessie agreed. Mark's horse had fallen during a wild chase only a few days ago. His mount had flipped completely over and Mark had separated a shoulder. One arm was in a sling and Jessie knew the injury was painful and needed at least a week of rest. "We may need fresh horses, but not for you. Mark, you are definitely not in any shape to ride!"

"I don't have any choice. I can break a couple of the smaller mustangs. My shoulder doesn't hurt that bad anyway."

"Yes it does," Ki said, stepping forward. "I'll ride, you shout instructions."

Chena looked worried and Jessie said, "Are you sure your own side is completely healed?"

"Yes," Ki answered confidently.

Jessie nodded. "Just be careful."

The mustang was big and stout, a bay with a white blaze down her face. She looked intelligent, but when Jessie's rope settled over her head she fought like crazy. With his one free hand, Mark grabbed her by the ear and twisted it hard while Ki cinched down his own saddle.

"Aren't we supposed to do this in a corral?"

"Yeah," Mark said with a thin smile. "Breaking broncs out on the range is just asking for trouble. Not only do you worry about staying seated, but you have to fear the animal stepping in a prairie-dog hole and landing upside down on you. It happens. Be careful."

"You're the second one that's said that," Ki observed dryly as he finished cinching the mustang and dropped the stirrup. "I will!"

Before anyone quite realized it, Ki swung into the saddle. The bay shot straight up to the sky and came down stiff-legged. Jessie saw Ki's neck snap like a whip. His chin struck his chest and his face drained of color. The mare spun and Ki grabbed for leather as the animal again launched itself at the sky.

Ki was not as skilled a horseman as men born to the West, but he was a natural athlete with perfect balance, timing, and coordination. Now, he substituted these attributes for experience and fought the bronc in a manner that was unorthodox but effective. He sat loose and his body absorbed the punishment like a veteran fighter who had learned how to roll with a punch. The harder the mustang bucked the better he seemed to adapt, and soon he was actually smiling.

Jessie chuckled. "Look, Mark, he's actually enjoying himself!"

When the mare gave up, Mark seemed a little disappointed. "Isn't there anything your friend can't do well?" he asked with a trace of vexation.

Jessie was proud enough of Ki to burst her buttons. "If there is," she said, "I haven't found out what it is yet."

Mark frowned. "Hell," he said, "give me a couple of more days and I'll show you what a real bronc buster can do in the saddle."

She winked. "I already know how good a rider you are."

Before he could recover and think of a rejoinder, Jessie was grabbing the defeated bay mare and shaking Ki's hand. "I get to try the next one."

Ki's mouth tightened at the corners with unspoken disapproval. He would never tell her she could not do a thing, but he worried about her like a father with his only child. And when he and Mark roped another mare, Jessie saw that it was not as big and strong. These men thought that she was fooled, but they were wrong. Almost nothing went by Jessica Starbuck that she didn't see and understand. She would allow them to give her this smaller mustang mare first, but the next one she broke would be equal to Ki's bay.

It snowed hard the day in late October when they caught their thousandth mustang. The early storm found them thundering toward the catch corral. Everyone, including Three Kills and his Indians, was so happy they gathered wood and had a huge bonfire that drove away the chilling cold.

"We've done it!" Jessie said, calling across the fire, which sizzled under falling snowflakes. "Chief Three Kills, I swear Mark and I will get you permission to buy title to a huge hunk of this land."

The Paiute beamed and when he translated that to the members of his tribe, they all cheered and laughed.

Jessie studied their weary, dirt-streaked faces. She would pay them ten thousand dollars before leaving Elko and would make sure that they were allowed to buy land, along with enough food and supplies to mustang on their own. Perhaps, when the drought that gripped this country ended, they would also buy sheep and cattle. No longer would the rumors persist that Three Kills and his tribe were a bloodthirsty bunch of scalpers.

*Everything we wanted to accomplish has been accomplished,* she thought proudly. *Now all we have to do is deliver the thousand head of mustangs and this saga will have ended.*

She could almost feel the luxury of the warm silk sheets and heavy down comforter that lay across her great oak bed at Circle Star. It was going to be very satisfying returning home to Texas.

Toro Montoya stood beside the corral of mustangs with his arm around the waist of a magnificently built woman. He had paid a man for the use of his cabin and corral that nestled ten miles west of Denver. To the east, he could look back on that bustling city resting on the edge of the Great Plains. He saw clear skies and a flat, tabletop land without contour. But to the west, the big-shouldered Rockies towered almost directly overhead. Toro's collar was turned up against an icy mountain wind. He could see immense thunderheads piling up on the highest peaks and his eyes followed the backbone of the Rockies northward clear into Wyoming.

"It's going to snow," he said to no one in particular. "I don't like snow or cold."

His men said nothing. A week in Denver's whore-houses and saloons had left them jaded, and they were almost eager to see action and drink clean water instead of whiskey. A few of them even admitted they thought it was about time they started earning their pay. But the lovely woman on Toro's arm pouted at the thought of a good-bye.

Her name was Carmen and she was tall, shaped like an hourglass, and possessed of a stunning face and figure. The men wondered if Toro had found her in a high-class brothel, or bought her from some bankrupt stage manager. She could sing like a nightingale and even the most cynical of them believed, when Toro played his guitar and Carmen sang a love song, that the pair could have become famous together. If she was as good— even half as good—in bed as she was in voice . . . well, a man might lose himself in her embrace and think he had been reborn in heaven.

"When will you return?" she asked softly, her dark eyes misted with sadness.

"Soon," he told her. "Soon, my darling."

"And you will take me with you to Mexico City,

where I will throw roses to my famous matador in the bullring?"

He laughed, fine white teeth flashing with pleasure. "If that pleases you, Carmen. Yes!"

The men shifted uneasily, but strained to hear the conversation without appearing to do so. Though none would have admitted it, they feared and admired Toro. Feared him because Paul had challenged Toro for Carmen's affections. That strong man had been carved to pieces by the bullfighter. Not one of them would ever forget the way Toro had moved, the subtleties of his fakes, and the calm, almost perfect thrusts designed to weaken and enrage. Toro's speed both of foot and hand had been unbelievable. When Paul had began to stagger about, half blinded with blood and with strips of flesh hanging off his torso, the hard-bitten American gunmen had interceded to ask Toro if he might end the torment. The bullfighter had granted their wish. He had allowed Paul to charge one last time and then had driven his blade deep, thrown his head back, and shouted, *"Olé!"*

The American gunmen had shivered, and the woman named Carmen had shivered too, but in a completely opposite way, and so violently that she had felt a hot wetness between her legs. That night, she had made love to Toro Montoya with such wild abandon that she feared she would never match it again.

Toro took the woman into the cabin now and used her once more before he had her bring him hot water for a bath. Afterward he selected a new set of clothes, shaved, and waxed the mustache that was his greatest vanity. If it were not for Jessica Starbuck, he might have taken Carmen with him back to that nothing town of Elko.

He kissed Carmen good-bye, promising on his honor to return soon, and then he mounted his horse and touched spurs, galloping toward Denver. Toro felt good. He knew that he could take however many new mustangs that Jessie, Ki, and Mark had managed to capture. And even if he had to kill the Starbuck woman along with her friends, he still had Carmen in waiting. A man could not do much better than that.

Jessie had no trouble this time making travel arrangements at the Central Pacific stockyards and train station. She was well remembered by the railroad-office manager and was delighted to hear that there was a train coming through the very next afternoon. Two days later, she and her mustangs would be in Denver to meet her Circle Star foreman, Ed Wright. Ed and her men would accompany them and the mustangs to the Mexican border.

Jessie left Ki with the mustangs to make sure they were properly fed. She and Mark immediately headed to the telegraph office. When the operator saw her, he dropped his pencil and licked his lips nervously. "Hello there, ma'am," he said in a voice that almost broke, "now look, I'm sorry—"

She interrupted him in midsentence. "I know what you're going to say, and it's all right. It doesn't matter."

He mopped his brow. Surely she must have learned that her previous telegrams had not been dispatched over the wires. "It . . . it doesn't?"

"No," she said. "An hour's delay isn't that important in this case."

Jessie scribbled out another message to Ed telling him she was on her way to Denver and giving him the estimated time of arrival. She wrote a second telegram to her banker in Texas, asking him to wire a return guarantee for eleven thousand dollars to the bank here in Elko. It would be a pleasure to pay Three Kills and his people ten thousand dollars; she would need the extra thousand for shipping and stockyard expenses both here and in Denver. She placed both messages in the wire basket, wondering why the telegraph operator was acting so nervous.

"Do you want to send a telegram to your father?"

Mark nodded. He penciled in a short message that all was well and they had one thousand mustangs. Because of secrecy, he did not say for whom.

The operator counted the words and they paid, then left.

"Nervous fella," Mark said when they got outdoors.

"Must be a bad day over the lines," Jessie said with a shrug of her shoulders. "Let's get a hotel room, and after I freshen up I want to see the sheriff."

Mark stopped in midstride. "Why? Do you think that the revolutionaries might try to hit us before we leave?"

"No, but it wouldn't hurt to ask if he has seen any new arrivals. What I really want to do is tell him all about Three Kills and his people. They need supplies and it is ridiculous that, now that they have money enough to buy land, they can't come in for food, blankets, and supplies. If the sheriff is a just man, he'll take it upon himself to protect those Indians and see that they are treated fairly."

"And if he isn't a just man?"

Jessie scowled. "I don't know. We'll cross that bridge if necessary."

"You'll figure out something," Mark said as they passed a tall, dark-complexioned man who smiled at Jessie and ignored Mark completely.

The man was so extraordinarily handsome and his eyes so penetrating as he studied Jessie that Mark glanced back over his shoulder. The fellow was entering the telegraph office, so Mark dismissed him from his mind.

Toro had eased open the telegraph operator's door so quietly he was unnoticed until he had read both of Jessie's telegraph messages and was about to read Mark's.

"Hold it!" the operator cried, leaping out of his chair and snatching the wire basket away to hug it to his chest. "You're the one that took them the last time! Admit you are!"

Toro shrugged with the feigned innocence of a child. "I don't know what you are talking about. I only want to send a message."

"No you don't! You came to steal Miss Starbuck's telegrams again!"

The smile on Toro's lips dissolved into a hard, uncompromising line. "Señor," he whispered, "are you calling me a liar?"

There was a smooth but decidedly deadly purr to his voice that had the equivalent warning of a diamondback's rattles. The telegraph operator looked into the coldest black eyes he had ever seen in his life and an alarm bell went off inside his shriveling heart.

"No . . . no sir!" he stammered. "I didn't say that! I just . . ." He swallowed noisily and thought about his wife and three children. "I just wanted to say that there will be a small delay. 'Bout an hour is all."

Toro favored him with the hint of a smile. "Very well," he said, thinking how ten thousand dollars might buy him enough protection to return to Spain if the Mexican revolution failed. "I will come back."

"Good!" the telegraph operator said much too loudly. "I mean, I'm glad you're not in a hurry. And if—"

But his words were terminated by the slamming of the door. Toro strolled back toward his room on Main Street at the Belmont Hotel. Jessie Starbuck would stay there, for it was the best of the three hotels the town had to offer. But so too would her friends, the New Mexico rancher and the dangerous man named Ki. Toro knew he had to use guile rather than guns while still in Elko.

He smiled with amusement and wondered if there was any way to also get that ten thousand dollars. Of course there was, he thought, since when had Toro Montoya never succeeded in parting money from a woman? Granted, this was no ordinary woman. Better if she were old or ugly—then he could easily charm her. No, he thought, the Starbuck woman would not be so easy to trick. But then, it was the difficult things in life that made victory the sweetest.

Toro saw a candy store and walked inside. A pretty young woman behind the counter smiled at him with unconcealed admiration. "May I help you?" she asked.

"You have already . . . with the gift of your smile," he said, adding just the right touch by caressing her eyes with his.

The girl blushed. Flustered, she became tongue-tied, and then suddenly very coquettish. Toro felt embarrassed for her and wished that he had a little time to teach her why a pretty girl, no matter how mean her circumstances or low her position in life, could charm any man, even a king. But then he thought of Jessie Starbuck and knew that he had no time for this girl and that the stakes he intended to play for were very high indeed.

"I'll take your largest and finest box of candy," he said with regret.

"For your . . . mother?"

"No," he replied almost sadly, "for a woman even more beautiful than you."

The candy-store clerk blinked, sighed, and managed to say, "That will be five dollars, sir."

Toro walked back out into the bright sun and headed swiftly toward the hotel. He would bathe, shave, change his clothes and present himself at the very first opportunity. One that would have to come this evening if it were not to be too late. The ten thousand dollars would no doubt be available by tomorrow.

It was a difficult and worthy challenge, but then, he had an entire night to give Miss Starbuck his complete attention. Surely, the prize and its beautiful owner would be his.

# Chapter 10

Jessie shook hands with the sheriff, her eyes measuring his integrity, or lack of it as the case might be. Sheriff Roy Morse was fiftyish and potbellied, his hair was silver, and he had a drinker's bulbous, red-veined nose. Yet his eyes were clear and direct, his office tidy, his desk uncluttered. She smelled no liquor on his breath and his hands did not shake. He might be one of the rare and lucky men who had escaped the hell of perpetual drunkenness.

In a few short words, she told the man about the plight of Three Kills and his Indians and how they had assisted her with the mustangs. She was careful to avoid any mention of Mexico, but instead intimated that the mustangs would be sold for slaughter.

"Well," Sheriff Morse said, "I've already heard about that first shipment you sent and we are damned glad to see 'em gone from this droughty country. Damned glad. You and the Indians have done a big favor for the ranchers. Big favor."

"Thank you. Now you can do Three Kills and his tribe a favor by letting them come into Elko and seeing that they are unharmed and unmolested when they shop for supplies. I would also ask that you do not allow your merchants to overcharge them, as has been done by many unconscionable merchants on the reservations."

"Well now, ma'am, lookee here, now. Those merchants largely pay my salary, such as it is. I can't—"

"You can and you should," Jessie interrupted. "What kind of salary do you earn each month?"

"Forty dollars, but—"

"I will supplement that with forty more if you give me your word that Three Kills and his people will be treated fairly in Elko."

"Well, hell yeah!" The man grinned. "For forty dollars extra, I'll make them redskins out a shopping list every time they come into town."

"They are Indians, Mr. Morse. Not redskins, or savages, or heathens. But Indians."

He held his hands up, palms out, in a gesture of peace. "No offense intended. I will protect them as long as they obey the laws of Elko."

"They might even open a sizable account at your local bank. Furthermore, I am going to tell you in advance that they will be buying a large piece of land south of here."

"Injuns ownin' land?"

"Indians! Not Injuns, dammit!"

"Yes, ma'am, but—"

Mark Lyon interrupted. "Don't ask, Sheriff. Just believe that we know the proper people in Washington, D.C., and that these Indians will own their own land."

The sheriff leaned back in his swivel chair and nodded agreeably. "Sizable money like yours always talks, Miss Starbuck. I believe what you say."

"Thank you." This man was bigoted and insensitive but he was not obtuse. Jessie had met good and bad lawman. She believed that, a long as her company paid this man forty dollars a month, he would be the friend of Three Kills and his tribesmen. If he were ever fired or killed in the line of duty, and he did not look like the sort who would take any chances where his life was concerned, she would send a representative to offer the same sort of deal to his replacement. It was very small money very well spent for a people that had been oppressed and misunderstood too long.

She rose to leave. "I will have the money deposited in your account tomorrow."

"Oh, no, please," he said quickly. "Ah, that would be . . ."

"I understand. It would raise questions you would not like to answer. The city council would not be pleased to know that Jessie Starbuck owned as much of your loyalty as I do. Is that it?"

"Yes, ma'am. I couldn't have said it better myself."

"Very well then, it will be sent to this office each month without a return address." She stopped in his doorway. "One more thing. Do you still drink heavily?"

He had been grinning when the question caught him by surprise and tore the grin from his thick lips. "I quit," he vowed, raising one hand like he was taking a pledge. "Swore off the stuff two years ago."

Now Jessie smiled. A drunk was not a man to be trusted—he would sell out the devil himself for a drink when his pockets were empty. It took character to quit the bottle. "Congratulations."

"Well, thank you, Miss Jessica Starbuck!" he hooted. "Thank you very, very much!"

They headed on down the boardwalk. Mark looked closely at her. "What do you think of him?"

"At forty dollars a month, he's a bargain."

The knock on her door surprised Jessie. She glanced at the clock on her dressing-room table. It was too early for Ki and Mark to arrive and escort her down to dinner. Jessie moved across the room in a silk dressing gown that was long and slinky. It clung to her shapely form and caressed her every contour and curve. She took her gun and walked over to the door.

"Who is it?"

"Hotel clerk with a an urgent telegram from Denver sent by a Mr. Ed Wright, Miss Starbuck."

She relaxed. Only someone legitimate would know her foreman's name and current whereabouts. That still did not mean she was taking any chances. "Read it to me, please."

"You'll have to sign for it, ma'am."

She cocked the gun. If there were any tricks to be given, she would give them, not the man who waited in the hallway.

When she opened the door, he was also holding a gun and it was pointed directly at her stomach. Jessie tried to slam the door shut, but he jammed his foot in the doorway and said, "Move and you are dead."

"So are you."

"Mexican standoff, ain't it," he growled. "Only difference is, I got nothing to lose and you got everything."

He was unshaven and smelled of horse and sweat. He had deep-set little eyes under a heavy shelf of overhanging bone. But he did have a fair point. Jessie was no more or less afraid to die than anyone else, but there were a lot of people who depended upon her and there was much good work left for her and Ki to do. *I will buy time*, she decided.

"I don't have much money with me in this room."

"How much?"

"A couple of hundred dollars."

"Lady, that's a goddamn fortune to a man like me. Get it and I'll skedaddle outa this town and say a prayer for you every night the rest of this year."

Jessie stared at his gun and at hers. She decided that two hundred dollars was not worth the risk of dying. At this range, they might both be mortally wounded. She opened the door and stepped back, her gun still trained on his stomach.

"Nice and easy, Miss Starbuck. Just back up to wherever the money is and hand it over nice and easy."

"All right." She began to back up, aware that his

attention was being distracted by the outline of her body against the silk dressing gown.

He swallowed hungrily. "God, but you're the finest-looking woman I ever saw in my life! I sure would—"

"Don't," Jessie said, her voice slicing like a cleaver. "Don't even say it. Just take the money and leave while you can."

"All right," he grated, nodding his head up and down.

Jessie found the money and came forward to give it to him. He snatched it away and then began to retreat toward the door. Jessie wondered if she could shoot him when he was going down the stairs. Possibly. But he was dressed so shabbily and the stairway was poorly lighted. It would be a shame to risk killing this man for that kind of money. Wounding, yes. She would have no qualms about wounding a thief, but not killing.

He was almost at the doorway when she caught a sudden movement in the hallway. All at once, a tall, very graceful man leapt at the thief's back and struck him a heavy blow. Her money fluttered to the floor and the thief tried to spin and fire his gun. He never had a chance. Two perfectly executed blows to his face sent him backpedaling into the room. Jessie reversed her grip and knocked the man cold with her pistol.

The man who had acted so gallantly moved like a cat and was strikingly handsome. "Beautiful woman," he said with a dashing smile, "what a wonderful happenstance that I should be passing your room with a box of chocolates when you needed me! The gods must favor us tonight! Why, and to think that I was taking a box of the finest candy to someone else not half so lovely."

Jessie smiled back at the man and watched him retrieve the box of candy, and present it to her with a slight bow. "You saved me two hundred dollars and are obviously gallant and a gentleman. Have you seen this man before?"

118

Toro Montoya stared down at the man he had employed to carry out this charade. The poor soul would probably receive a six-month jail sentence for attempted robbery but he had been paid well for his impending captivity. "No, I have never seen the scoundrel before in my life. I will call the sheriff at once."

"Call the hotel desk. They'll send for Sheriff Morse." They shared some chocolate. While it was nothing like what you could get in Switzerland or even New York City, it was very good for the West. "You really know how to use your fists. And you speak with a faint but very nice foreign accent. You are Spanish, is this not so?"

Her guess startled Toro. He had been gauged Italian, Mexican, Egyptian, Basque, French, and even Brazilian, but rarely of Spanish descent.

"Yes, how did you guess?"

"I have an office in Madrid and Spain is one of my favorite European countries."

His eyebrows lifted. "I see, then we have much to talk about! Oh, Señorita, if you knew how I hunger for my own country! But I am here by the wishes of the King of Spain. Tomorrow, I go to Denver."

"So do I," Jessie said happily.

He clapped his hands together. "Truly, the gods favor me tonight! We will have much time to speak to each other of many things."

Jessie could not help but be attracted to him. He was a magnificent specimen of manhood and there was much she wanted to ask him about Spain. Which were its finest castles, its best land for wine, and did he think that the black Spanish fighting bulls could be bred with the American longhorns? And if so, what kind of an animal would be produced?

"Would you like a drink, Sénor...?"

"Montoya," he told her truthfully, because he had learned that mixing names was like mixing drinks or

119

mixing women—you soon became confused and forgetful and that led to great distress. "Toro Montoya."

"Unusual name," she said.

"I am an unusual man," he replied. He stepped into the hallway and called down to the hotel desk. A few minutes later, men hustled upstairs and the thief was dragged downstairs and hauled off to jail.

For the next forty-five minutes, they talked of many things, and of nothing at all. He was, she quickly discovered, a brilliant conversationalist, witty, well-educated, and very refined. He had an excellent sense of humor and was highly entertaining. It had been years since Jessie had met so charming and well-traveled a man.

The knock at her door surprised them both and then Jessie remembered. "I had forgotten I was to be escorted to dinner by my friends Ki and Mark."

He looked crestfallen. "There is room service. Allow me the honor of your company and I will order us a wonderful dinner and champagne to celebrate the job we did on your thief. Surely you would not break my heart and leave me now."

"You could join us."

He shook his head sadly. "After basking alone in your beauty, I would wilt with jealousy if I had to share your company with other men. Please, Señorita. Let me order a small dinner so we can be alone."

Jessie found she had lost her appetite. She also discovered that, since she had shared every evening for months with Ki and Mark, the idea of sharing just one with this exciting man was very pleasant indeed. "Very well," she whispered.

She opened the door a crack and both Mark and Ki could see that she was not dressed. Jessie quickly explained and ended by saying, "I'm afraid I have lost my appetite. Please go without me. I'll see you in the morning."

Mark was openly disappointed, but Ki only nodded. He knew she was not alone and he probably even realized the cause of her loss of appetite. She and Ki understood each other very well whenever lovers were involved. They both shared the normal desires of healthy men and women and respected each other's right to privacy and freedom to choose their sexual partners.

"I will not be far," Ki said, letting her know that, if there was any trouble whatsoever, he would be close and ready to help.

"I'll be fine. Go enjoy a well-deserved dinner not cooked over a campfire's ashes."

She closed and locked the door. When Toro saw the hungry look in her eyes, the sway of her provocative hips, and heard the tumblers of her door fall, he felt himself harden with sexual excitement. This woman was a love goddess! A moment ago, he had actually been thinking of ordering a meal. No longer. Miss Starbuck would be his meal. She and the chocolates that would give them both the strength to make love through a long and passionate night.

When she crossed the room toward him, he moved to enfold her in his arms. They seemed to understand that the time for small talk was later. Their lips touched softly at first, then with more pressure and urgency until they embraced in a swaying pillar of passion.

"Your bed," he whispered, leading them over to it and laying her down gently. Without breaking their kiss, they sank down on the thick bed cover, and Toro's expert hands began to brush the silken fabric of her dressing gown, sending Jessie into shivering desire. His lips pulled from hers and traced their way down to the soft curve of her throat, and then his fine teeth nibbled playfully at her earlobe.

She felt his hand cup her breast and then move down until it came to the source of her greatest heat. The gown was twisted tightly against her body and even

Toro was stymied for a moment as to how to reach her womanhood.

"I think we have too many barriers between us," she told him, not wanting his lean, muscular body to leave her own, but knowing it must.

"I agree," he whispered. He stood and watched as she slipped out of the dressing gown, and when he saw the fullness of her beauty, he sighed with anticipation and reached for his belt buckle.

"Let me," she told him, coming off the bed and unbuttoning his shirt. Jessie's hands touched his smooth, dark skin and she saw it ripple like that of a lion. "What is this?"

"An old wound," he said, remembering how the bull had gored him when he was but a thin boy of seventeen and dizzy with the hot Spanish sun. He had been thrown high in the air like a rag doll, but had managed to climb to his feet and make the kill. It was one of his greatest victories, but also one of the most costly. He had been near death for a month.

"You must have been shot at close range by a blunderbuss or small cannon," she said, kissing the huge scar near his heart. Jessie's hands slipped down and she loosened his pants and then pushed them over his hips. When her fingers touched his throbbing manhood, she was astonished by his size.

"Now I think I know why they call you Toro," she said in a voice thick with passion.

He laughed and they tumbled back onto the bed, Toro's mouth and tongue working at first one of her nipples, then the other.

"I want you now!" she whispered urgently, her legs opening wide and the fire between them so hot she writhed with eagerness.

"There is no hurry, Señorita Starbuck," he whispered, but he moved over her and she felt the huge tip of him probing.

Jessie reached down and grabbed him, then began to

122

rub his stiff erection back and forth over the lips of her womanhood until she was bubbling with love juices and ready to receive all of him. Her hips lifted and she guided him into her and then gasped with pleasure as he thrust and penetrated her wet, swollen cavern.

"Ohhh," she moaned, her hips rocking up to meet his, her hands reaching around behind to grasp his buttocks and pull him as deep as any man had ever been, "Ohhh, Toro, take me quickly!"

Toro was a man who loved to slowly drive a woman wild with his great skill and size, but this one made him lose control. He could not wait to fill her with his seed, and soon his rapid thrusting matched her own. He tried mightily to slow his body but it was out of control, and so he gave into the pure, animal joy of coupling and set the beast in him free.

"Yes, Jessica!" he shouted, pistoning in and out, feeling the woman's insides milking him wildly. "Yes, now!"

They rose on a heaving sea of passion that carried them ever higher. Jessie knew they were both going to scream and so her mouth covered his. Finally, their bodies locked and spasmed with an explosive climax that spiraled them upward in muffled cries of heavenly insanity.

It took them some time to catch their breath and when Jessie looked into Toro's eyes, the hidden guardedness she had noticed before was gone. "You are the most beautiful and talented woman I have ever had," he said truthfully. "You are like an opiate, a man could never get enough of you. Once taken, he would give anything to love you again and again."

Jessie smiled. She had sensed this man had been supremely confident of his artistry in bed, and he had a right to be. But she had never met any man she could not consume in his own fire and Toro Montoya was no exception.

She began to use the muscles of her womanhood and

they squeezed and coaxed new life into his great shaft. "Tonight," she said, "you may have all you want of me and I of you. But tomorrow, my dear, wonderful lover, tomorrow I cannot promise you anything. In Denver, you must go your way, and I mine."

He nodded, for it was true, and he tried to tell himself that, after tonight, she would still love him even after he stole her mustangs and her money. But that was a dream. Toro knew that this woman would hate and want to kill him. She was too strong ever to be tamed by a man who had betrayed her in love.

This filled him with sadness and, for the first time in years, he made love with such great beauty and tenderness that it surprised even himself.

# Chapter 11

Jessie kissed Toro good-bye just before sunrise and went back to sleep for a few hours. When she awoke, she took a bath and felt completely refreshed. She had never met a man quite like Toro. He was one of the best lovers she had ever known. The Spaniard had the capacity to be both tender and wildly passionate.

But something had not been exactly right about the man. As she dressed, Jessie tried to put her finger on what it was about Toro that troubled her. She finally decided it was that he had been unusually vague about his past and could give her no satisfactory reason for his being sent to this country by the King of Spain. During one conversation, he had professed not to be a aficionado of the bullring, and yet, when she mentioned the name of a current and very famous Spanish matador, his voice had filled with scorn. "The man is nothing! A buffoon!"

Jessie wondered if Toro might possibly be connected with the revolutionaries. After all, hadn't Mark been expecting danger? But if Toro was an agent of Armando Escobar, then why hadn't he tried to charm information out of her? A true revolutionary spy would have wanted to know something about the mustangs and the number of men who would be waiting in Denver to help her receive them. Toro had asked her nothing. He had not tried to create a bond of love so he might be extended an invitation into her home and business interests, as had many a smooth-talking and handsome opportunist.

No, she thought, Toro can't be a revolutionary spy, nor is he just a handsome parasite seeking the warmth of my fire and fortune. He had left saying only that he hoped he would be welcome to share both her delightful company and that of her friends on the train ride to Denver.

Jessie finished dressing and left her room locked securely. She hurried downstairs, where Ki and Mark were waiting for her to join them for breakfast.

"I'm famished," she said, meaning it.

They both studied her with blank faces. If Mark was angry or jealous, he was smart enough not to show it. They were served a delicious breakfast, which Jessie devoured, and then they left to inspect the mustangs.

"Please," Jessie said, "stay here and watch over the mustangs for us. Ki and I will stop by the bank for Three Kills' money. If we ride out within the hour, we should easily return by two o'clock."

"And if you don't," Mark said, clearly unhappy with the arrangements that left him to stay at the stockyard. "What then?"

"Load the mustangs and go on ahead to Denver."

"But if you don't return, how am I to know you haven't been ambushed? Ten thousand dollars is a hell of a lot of money to go riding off with."

Jessie appreciated his concern, but she and Ki were perfectly capable of protecting themselves. "It is fairly open country," she said. "And we will be careful."

"I don't like it," Mark fumed. "But I'll do it."

"Thank you. I talked again to the sheriff about Three Kills coming in for supplies with us. Everything will be fine, so please stop worrying."

Jessie and Ki mounted their horses outside the bank and galloped out of town, heading for a camp about ten miles east where the Indians were waiting. As they rounded the corner of Main Street, Toro Montoya stepped out of the barber shop and waved farewell to them. One half of his jaw was covered with shaving cream and the other side was shiny and smooth as a baby's skin. Both sides of his mouth were lifted in a smile.

Five miles out of town all his best riflemen were hidden in ambush. There were under the strictest orders to shoot Ki and allow Jessie to escape unharmed after relieving her of the money. Toro took a deep breath. If they somehow failed—and he was sure they would not —it would be remembered that he had been getting a fresh shave on Main Street. Any suspicions that Jessie might have about his complicity would be erased, and he still had another half-dozen men who were going to be boarding the eastbound train carrying the mustangs for Mexico. No matter what happened out there on the range, the mustangs now belonged to him. And if everything went as expected, he would rush to Jessie's aid and completely ingratiate himself with her.

He would sympathize with her concerning the loss of her Oriental friend and her money. Perhaps she would reward him in ways he could not even imagine. They would have to wait for the next eastbound train, and by then she would be totally under his control. Meanwhile, his men would have killed the New Mexico rancher and taken this new band of mustangs to join the others outside of Denver.

*I can have it all,* he thought, feeling very proud of himself. *The woman, the money, and the rest of the mustangs.* It was a rather brilliant plot. *Maybe,* he thought, *I should have become a Spanish general. Perhaps after I finish my career as a bullfighter, I will seek a military commission in Escobar's new armies. General Toro Montoya—yes, I like the ring of it!*

Ki glanced at Jessie and wondered about her thoughts. Was she still thinking about the man she had made love to last night, or was her mind on the Indians and the days that lay ahead, when they would bring the valuable horses to the government of Mexico? He had looked at the man Jessie had slept with last night when he had emerged from the barber shop. Just a passing glance as their horses shot past, but enough for a man trained to see and observe to form an intelligent opinion. Toro Montoya was too . . . Ki almost wanted to use the word pretty, and yet there was enough iron in his face and body to make the word inappropriate. The man had seemed too self-assured and self-centered. Yes, that was it. Ki had seen at a glance that he was dressed quite expensively, but also that his clothes, boots, and suit were showy. Ki did not admire peacocks and, for that reason, he did not trust Jessie's lover.

They had little time to spare and so they rode hard, Ki lost in his thoughts, Jessie in her own.

Twenty minutes later, when riflemen suddenly appeared and opened fire, Ki had barely enough time to fling himself from his horse with a shouted warning to Jessie. They hit the ground rolling and kept their heads down as a swath of bullets chopped the brush overhead.

"Are you all right?" Ki asked.

"Yes, and you?"

Ki nocked an arrow and began to crawl forward. He was already within shooting range for an arrow, but he preferred to be closer. Jessie had not had time to pull her rifle from its scabbard, but she was armed with her pistol.

They could hear the thundering hoofbeats of their own horses as they raced across the hard-packed ground. "I think," Jessie said, drawing her pistol and crawling after Ki, "that we are going to miss our train to Denver."

Ki allowed himself to smile. He never failed to appreciate how courageous Jessie Starbuck was under fire. She was like her father had been, at her best with her back to the wall. Jessie was a woman worth fighting and dying beside.

128

Their ambushers were fanning out into a wide horse-shoe-shaped line, the men at the ends trying to circle around behind. Ki saw their plan and motioned to Jessie, who followed him toward the men nearest. He waited until she was beside him and then he indicated that she should crawl off a short distance and be ready to fire.

Ki waited until she was ready. He jumped to his feet and released an arrow that hummed across a flat trajectory and buried itself in a rifleman's chest. The man screamed and crashed into the brush, and Jessie's gun banged out two shots that sent another ambusher down. Before the others could react, Ki swiveled around and another arrow was nocked in his bowstring. He drew it back and fired, then ducked, knowing his arrow would find its target.

Bullets laced the air over his head and he heard a scream as his target died with an arrow through his lungs.

"Three down," Ki said. "I think we can go after them now without worry."

"Overconfidence can be fatal, Ki. They still have Winchesters."

Ki knew he was not being overconfident, and yet he could not take the slightest chance where Jessie's life was concerned. So he stayed low and they began to crawl back toward the other flank. When he raised his head, the ambushers were gone.

"I don't see them," he said.

"Could they have run so soon?"

"I don't think so. Listen."

They held their breath in silence, and presently they heard the breaking of a stick nearby. Jessie spun around and flattened to the earth. She caught sight of movement and took careful aim through the heavy brush. When the face of a man appeared, she squeezed the trigger. The rifleman's face vanished and she heard the sound of his body as it fell in death.

129

Ki killed the fifth man with a perfect shot, but the sixth was so close he used one of his deadly *shuriken* star-blades. When the last man raised his rifle to finish Ki, Jessie had to snap off a hurried shot from hip level, but placed it cleanly through the ambusher's brain.

Ki was impressed enough to say, "Very nice snap shooting, Jessie."

"No, it wasn't. I was aiming for the man's shoulder. I wanted to take one of them alive so we could find out who tipped them off that we were coming out here."

"Did you tell your friend?"

"No," Jessie said. "It might have been the sheriff."

"Or the banker or telegraph operator. They all knew about the money you received today. And I'll bet they each told many different people."

Jessie understood what he was saying. There was no way to tell who had instigated this ambush. Anyone could have done so, anyone except Toro Montoya, she thought happily, because she had kept him busy almost all night long.

"We've got a long walk ahead of us," Jessie sighed, not seeing any horses, though she knew the ambushers had to have hidden theirs somewhere.

"No we don't," Ki said, his eyes catching a rising cloud of dust that grew larger as a body of horsemen approached.

"It's Three Kills and most of his tribe—and they've got our horses!"

"And their money," Ki added.

The Indians stopped and dismounted. Jessie went to her horse, untied her bulging saddlebags, and handed them to Three Kills, saying, "I was going to open a bank account for you, but I changed my mind. It's your money to keep wherever you want."

"Thank you. I will use this to buy land when you send a man to say it can be done."

"He will come from Washington, D.C., before the

new year," she promised.

"Thank you for saving my people."

"Come back with us and buy food and supplies. I have talked to the sheriff and he swears to protect you from harm."

Three Kills looked toward Elko with a thoughtful gaze. At last, he nodded and ordered his hungry people to mount up, for they were going into the cattlemen's town.

Chena reined her pony in beside Ki. They rode in silence for a few minutes before she whispered, "I wish you long life and happiness. Also, a good woman of your own who will bear you sons."

Ki studied her openly. Chena herself could be such a woman and he was tempted to tell her that he might return someday and . . . and what? Break his sworn oath to protect Jessie Starbuck? Never! And even if Jessie were killed by their enemies, Ki knew that he would commit *seppuku*, the act of ritual disembowelment which was required of a samurai who had failed his sworn duty.

"You will find a man better to love than I," he told her, hoping this was true.

"I do not think so."

"Try. Chena, give me your word of honor that you will not seal your heart from the man who would open it like a flower in springtime."

The halfbreed girl struggled but finally nodded. "My word of honor," she managed to say.

"Thank you," he told her. "You make me very proud to have known you."

Their arrival in Elko created nothing less than a full-blown panic in Elko. Men and women shouted and raced for cover, certain that the town was about to be attacked by the Indians. Some fool fired a shot and Jessie cried. "Take cover!"

Ki leapt from his horse and sprinted down the street, shouting, "Hold your fire!"

Jessie managed to get the Indians back around the corner to safety. She was furious, and when Three Kills ordered his frightened women and children to retreat south while he and his men guarded their rear, Jessie knew that she had to stop the man. If Three Kills and his tribe were run out of town now, they would be hounded into eventual extinction.

"Please," she begged. "Let us talk to those people! I had assumed that the sheriff had passed the word around about your visit, but it's clear that he hasn't. We can make this town understand that you and your people come in peace."

Three Kills was stiff with rage. "They will never understand," he hissed. "The whites cannot be trusted."

Jessie blinked. "What about me? I'm white. Are you saying I lied about paying your people ten thousand dollars in cash for your mustangs? Or that Mark Lyon and I won't come through on our promise to see that you are allowed to buy title to your own land?"

The chief's rugged face softened. "I am sorry," he said at last. "I was wrong to doubt you. Talk to them. Tell them that my people have money to buy their goods and that we wish to live in peace with the whites."

Jessie nodded. She remounted and rode back down the street, where an angry crowd had gathered around the sheriff and Ki. Both men were trying to explain that the Indians had come in peace and that Three Kills was not a murderer or scalper.

Toro Montoya was standing on the boardwalk and, when he saw Jessie ride up, he stepped out onto the street. He was wearing a dark-brown suit and his shoes were polished to a luster. Tall, graceful, and self-assured, he looked like a hero on the cover of a dime-store novel, except that he was dark and dangerous.

"I think you need help," he said, falling in beside her

as they came to the angry crowd that was growing larger by the moment and threatening violence.

"Thank you," Jessie said, meaning it.

Toro drew his gun, raised it, and fired off three fast shots into the air. Some men scattered, others hit the dirt, but most, seeing the tall man's upraised arm, fell into silence.

"The beautiful *señorita* has something to say," Toro shouted. "And you will all listen."

Jessie had remained on her horse. And now, as she studied the hate-filled expressions of these townsmen, she wondered whether or not any words could persuade them that Three Kills and his tribe were no threat.

"There is a saying that the only good Indian is a dead Indian," she began.

"Makes damn good sense to me," a bull-necked man shouted, "I say, let's—"

Whatever he was about to say never left his lips, for Ki stepped in close and grabbed him. For a moment they strained against one another, and then Jessie saw Ki's fingers reach for the man's throat. Instead of choking him, the fingers expertly sought and found the *atemi* point and applied pressure. The man shuddered and dropped like a stunned animal, his brain momentarily shut off from its supply of blood.

Everyone gasped and drew back, staring at Ki with shock and wonder.

"What did that Chinaman do to Luke?" a man shouted.

The doctor stepped forward and knelt beside the prostrate man. After checking his pulse, he turned his head up to Ki and said, "How long will he be unconscious, and how did you do that so skillfully?"

Ki shifted uncomfortably, for he had never liked attention. "He will revive within fifteen minutes. It is an art I learned, and it sometimes proves useful to silence stupidity."

The doctor smiled. He said to the crowd, "Folks, Luke here is taking a short nap. Anyone else like to do the same? I'd sure appreciate seeing the Chinaman do this once more."

"He is not a Chinaman," Jessie said, "and there will be no violence this day. The Indians are friendly and have money to buy food and supplies."

"But that's Three Kills!" the town blacksmith protested loudly. "The sonofabitch didn't get his name by rocking a papoose!"

Jessie told them about the Paiute chief, how he had been raised by missionaries and saved a white woman from being murdered. And how, later, he had been forced to kill three thieving miners to protect her once again. "That's how he got his name. Protecting a woman who had come to love him. He wants to live in peace and he will keep mustanging so the wild horses that are stripping the range of forage will not overpopulate once more. Let him and his people live in peace and everyone benefits—make war on him and you will answer for it with a prison sentence."

She looked right at the sheriff of Elko and it was clear she expected him to back her to the hilt.

Sheriff Morse cleared his throat and then bellowed, "I mean to arrest anyone that causes trouble over those Indians or cheats them. And I have talked to the judge, who assures me that violence and lawlessness will not be tolerated. Kill one of 'em, you'll likely go to the gallows. Hurt, rape, or whip one, you may be killed in self-defense and, if not, you'll go to prison. Is that understood?"

"Look, here they come again!"

The crowd pivoted and saw Three Kills leading his people back onto the street. They fell silent and watched as the Paiutes came forward, until they were separated by less than ten yards. The chief dismounted, and his presence calmed the nervous whites, for he did not look wild or bloodthirsty at all.

134

"We are hungry but ask only to buy food," Three Kills said, eyes searching their faces. "Our blankets are thin and we are cold. Who will sell us food and blankets?"

"I will," the town's largest merchant blurted out loudly. "And I'll give you a discount for volume the same as I would anybody!" He shot a quick, defiant glance toward the other merchants, who looked ashamed because, up close, it was painfully clear how thin and ragged these people were.

The Methodist minister stepped forward and said, "In the name of my congregation, we welcome you, Chief Three . . . Three Kills. Won't you come to our church hall, where we can give the women and children some hot soup and a little candy?"

Not to be outdone, the Catholic priest volunteered his parish as well. Magically, the atmosphere of dark hatred and suspicion evaporated, and when Luke woke up a few minutes later, the Paiutes were mixing with the whites and several of the other merchants were offering some pretty nice buys of their own.

Ki was smiling and so was Toro Montoya. Jessie heard a train whistle and then saw the Central Pacific locomotive huffing out of the western horizon. It was time to start thinking about getting the mustangs ready to be loaded for the trip to Denver.

But one thing was sure. She could leave knowing that the sheriff and the people of Elko were going to treat the Paiutes just like neighbors.

Toro took her arm and slipped it through his. Jessie let him escort her back to the hotel. There were still a few hours before the train would be loaded and ready to start east with the mustangs.

Jessie wanted this man again.

# Chapter 12

The train had carried them out of Nevada and across the Great Salt Lake desert, where a cold, buffeting headwind had slowed their speed. The coaches rocked back and forth and sometimes the smoke from the locomotive would be whipped along the passenger cars and become extremely noxious. Jessie was very worried about their six boxcars of mustangs. The poor animals were packed in so tightly that, if one grew weak and fell, it would be trampled by the others.

Whenever the train had stopped on its long, gradual ascent toward the rugged Wasatch Mountains, Jessie, Ki, and Mark had rushed down and tried to feed and water their mustangs before the train began to roll eastward again. They were having little success. What the mustangs really needed was to be unloaded overnight and allowed enough time to eat and drink properly.

Jessie had spoken to the conductor and then the engineer, but they remained inflexible. The train had a timetable and, because of the headwind, they were already running late. To make matters even worse, it began to snow as they began their steep climb into the Wasatch Mountains, which would deliver them into southwestern Wyoming.

Jessie shook her head. "If we hit a blizzard," she said to the three men seated in the dining car with her, "there are probably at least fifty mustangs that are not strong enough to survive."

136

"We have no choice," Mark said.

Ki nodded. "If the storm comes down lower and we try to take shelter we might be caught without enough feed and lose hundreds before the weather cleared."

"I know," Jessie said with resignation. "I had hoped that we could get to Denver before something like this happened."

"Maybe the storm will not be so bad," Toro said. They could all see the sky up ahead, and suddenly everything in view disappeared in a sheet of swirling white.

"I wonder if this train ever gets snowed to a standstill?" Jessie asked, nervous at the thought of being stranded somewhere in the high mountains and watching their precious mustangs starve or freeze to death packed into those boxcars.

"I will find out," Toro said, rising and excusing himself. "I need to stretch my legs anyway."

"Thank you," Jessie said with a grateful smile.

Ki watched the man move down the aisle toward the rear of the train. Why did the Spaniard not go forward to the front of the train? It was an interesting question. They had been traveling together for almost twenty-four hours and Ki still found himself wondering about the handsome stranger that Jessie had taken to. Earlier this afternoon, the man had disappeared for several hours and, without seeming to, Ki had searched for him up and down the train without success. Toro had not retired to his own sleeping quarters, but had vanished.

"I think I will take a walk myself," Ki said innocently. He did not wish to speak to Jessie of his distrust yet.

"Will you check on the horses?" Jessie hated to ask because it meant climbing up on the roofs of the stockcars and peering down into them.

"Of course." Ki headed down the aisle, appearing very relaxed. He moved through a succession of

137

coaches, feeling the train slow as it entered a series of switchbacks and started to battle its way into the high Wasatch Mountains.

Ki passed through four second-class coaches full of miners, cowboys, and working-class people. Toro was nowhere to be found. There was only one passenger car left and now Ki peeked through its sooty window and saw Toro and a body of hard-looking gunmen deep in conversation.

Ki stood on the outside platform of the car, scarcely feeling the biting, wind-driven snow. Once, Toro glanced his way, but Ki did not think the man had time to notice him. A few minutes later, Toro and his men left their coach and exited into the storm by the opposite doorway. Ki knew that the next six cars were loaded with mustangs. After that, all that remained of the train was a car for baggage and mail followed by a caboose. Why were seven or eight men going into the freezing weather? To rob the baggage and mail? A distinct possibility.

Ki knew it was his first duty to alert Jessie and Mark to danger. There was no acute urgency, because no one was going anywhere. A man afoot would most likely die of exposure in the storm before he could find food or shelter.

When Ki returned to Jessie and Mark, he explained what he had seen and ended by saying, "Jessie, the man is not what he seems. Montoya knew those gunmen well. They must be train robbers. Maybe they have also been hired to steal the mustangs by the enemies of President González."

Jessie looked away, feeling the anger in her build. She did not want to admit that she might have been tricked. "Toro has shown no interest in the mustangs."

"Perhaps not, but no one would ever climb onto those ice-topped cattle cars without a very good reason."

138

"All right," Jessie said, knowing that Ki was correct to be suspicious. "Let's go find out what they're doing."

Jessie led the way. She tried to think of some reason why Toro would be consorting with a bunch of gunmen. He did not seem to be the kind of man who would rob trains. And yet, the only other possibility was that he was being employed by the Mexican revolutionaries to steal their Nevada mustangs. Jessie Starbuck was not in the habit of allowing anyone to deceive her and when, in rare instances, her judgment was inaccurate, she acted with swift decisiveness.

They moved through the train casually enough not to generate concern on the part of the other passengers. When they finally arrived at the platform outside the last coach, Jessie peered through the window. "He's not back yet."

"Then Ki and I had better go find him," Mark said. "You could wait here, Jessie."

"I'm going." She was not about to duck trouble.

Ki spoke. "One of us must stay to warn the conductor and engineer of possible danger to the entire train. The men I saw looked as though they might be capable of anything, Jessie. Please allow us to do this. We are dressed better for the freezing cold. Also, if there is a train robbery taking place, the conductor would obey you but not us."

"All right," Jessie finally allowed, aware that they were dressed much heavier and that she was the best choice to remain behind. "But if I hear gunshots or you aren't back in fifteen minutes, I'm coming."

"Agreed."

Ki moved swiftly through the last coach and then outside. The platform was slick with ice and the snow was swirling heavily, but at least there were climbing ladders. The cattle cars themselves had been constructed with solid siding and a roof, necessary to protect stock from this kind of mountain weather. Once on top, Ki found the wind and the cold to be murderous. The car swayed precariously. They both grabbed the hand-brake wheel for support. It took them a few moments to adjust to the train's rocking motion. A heavy cable ran along the center of each car and Ki saw the tracks of Toro and his men where they had passed but a few minutes earlier. It was impossible to see more than one car length in the blizzardlike conditions.

Ki started forward in a crouched position rather than on his hands and knees. Behind him, he heard Mark shout, but the rancher's words were snatched away in the wind. Ki slowed to allow the rancher to catch up. Every fifteen feet they came to an observation hole where they could look down into the car and observe the mustangs. They were all on their feet, but huddled together, heads down and steam rising from their nostrils. Ki had never seen a more pathetic lot of horses.

"Be thankful," Ki told them. "At least you are inside and wearing a very warm horsehair coat."

Then he thought of something else. Out here in this hard and swirling wind, his *shuriken* would be nearly useless. It was a good thing, Ki thought, that a samurai-trained warrior did not have to rely on any weapons except those of his hands and feet.

It seemed to take forever to traverse the six stockcars and reach the mail-and-baggage coach. Ki's face was numb and the snow-driven wind made his eyes blink tears that froze on his cheeks. He could tell that Toro and his men had not jumped across and continued on to the caboose. No, they had climbed down the icy ladder and entered the mail-and-baggage coach. Ki had expected this. There was only one thing that would force men to risk their lives crossing six snow-covered cattle cars, and that was the prospect of robbing the train's vault.

The mail-and-baggage coach was usually protected by armed guards. When Ki and Mark dropped down to the outside platform, they huddled in the swirling snow and discovered that the door's lock had been shot to pieces. Conversation between them was impossible but unnecessary; Ki figured that Mark understood what they faced inside.

Ki waited until Mark had his gun out from under his heavy coat and then he grabbed the busted door handle and threw his shoulder to the wood. Ki went through the door in a rush and, in the instant that he had to size up things, he saw Toro Montoya reaching for his gun. There were at least six other men inside and they were emptying the vault. Ki sent a sweep-lotus kick that knocked the gun spinning. A second man yelled a be-lated warning and started to spin around, but Ki slashed him with a *migi-shote* blow, using the heavily muscled edge of his stiffened hand.

Mark's gun boomed twice. One train robber dropped, but another was knocked spinning, and Toro used him as a shield as he brought another gun up and leveled it.

"Freeze!" Toro ordered.

There was no way that Ki could reach the Spaniard, shielded by another man's body, without being shot. His hands were up and tensed to strike, but now he lowered them, saying, "Put your gun away, Mark."

"But he'll—"

"Put it away," Ki ordered, tasting the acrid smell of gunsmoke in the packed coach. "He has the advantage."

"You're right," Toro said with a smile. "And if this gun in my hand isn't enough, back in the dining car one of my men has orders to take Miss Starbuck hostage if I don't return."

"You'd have her shot!" Mark bellowed in fury.

Toro hardly glanced at the rancher. "Of course not," he said with disgust. "I'm not a woman-killer. But she is my ace in the hole. I'm afraid you two have been outmatched and outwitted."

"Not entirely," Ki said. "I told her of my suspicions. She wanted to come, but agreed to wait. She would have caught on to your deception sooner or later. You will find her a worthy opponent."

"I expected she would be. However, in just another week, she wouldn't have cared if I was the devil himself."

Mark laughed with contempt. "Mister, you overestimate yourself!"

Rather than argue the point, Toro just smiled. Ki had the feeling that the man did not overestimate himself all that much. He was cocky and arrogant, sure. But he was also very, very capable and extremely clever. There was only one doubt in Ki's mind, and that was whether or not the man was a cold-blooded killer—someone capable of executing an opponent. Ki gambled with his life that the man was not.

"What are you going to do with us?" he asked.

"What would you do?" Toro shot back.

"That is of no importance."

"Let's kill him!" one of the wounded outlaws grated thickly as he struggled for his own weapon.

The gun in Toro's hand cocked ominously. "No," he said, "we do not need to do that. Let them die of natural causes. There will be no questions asked if they are found frozen to death."

"But—"

"Silence!" Toro shouted. "Or else you will join them out in the blizzard. My orders from Mexico were to avoid killing or raising a great deal of publicity.

Mark lifted his gun and pointed it at Toro. "You are going to die with me," he said. "I'm not jumping off this train in these mountains."

Toro's black eyes flicked to meet those of Ki. "Tell him to drop his gun because, if I am shot, these men will surely kill Miss Starbuck. I am the only thing that keeps them from stealing the locomotive and leaving all the passengers snowbound."

"Mark, drop your gun," Ki ordered.

Toro released the man he had been using as a shield.

142

The outlaw was hurt bad and sagged to the floor.

Ki looked at his bloodless face and then at the other wounded outlaws before his eyes returned to Toro's. "Are you going to throw all the wounded out, too? If so, they will be dead men long before dark."

Everyone looked at Toro. A decision had to be made and, normally, with hired gunmen such as this who neither expected nor gave mercy, the answer was clear— let them die.

Toro struggled inside. He had no love for these men and yet, he had never before killed without passion. To kill in battle, that was to do so with honor, but there was only shame in pushing wounded men out of a train to freeze in a snowbank. But neither could he afford to leave them on the train, for their bullet wounds would demand immediate medical attention and that would bring further questions, probably even a lawman.

Toro took a deep breath. Suddenly, he knew the answer. "Everyone out," he ordered. "Those of you not strong enough to crawl back across those six cattle cars will remain here. We uncouple this coach and the caboose and leave. There won't be a train through for days, and by then we will be in southern Colorado with all the mustangs."

"Boss, if we kill them, then—"

"Outside," Toro snapped. "There is no need for killing. Besides, with wounded men to care for, they must stay with the train until they either starve or help arrives. The samurai and his idealistic friend are too civilized to abandon our friends. Isn't that right, Ki?"

Ki did not answer. He watched as the outlaws gathered up the bags of money and valuables taken from the train vault. One by one, they exited from the front of the coach until only Toro stood on the swaying platform. The Spaniard was smiling, the snow already forming a mantle of white on his coal-black hair. "I wish you well, Ki and Mark," he called through the wind.

Mark cursed as they heard the coupling pin being wrenched free. The coach and caboose almost seemed to stumble as their forward momentum was arrested. Toro waved good-bye and then his smiling, handsome face disappeared as the train carried him away in the whiteness.

Ki leapt forward, but even before he reached the platform he could see that the last cattle car, with Toro hanging on its rear ladder, was thirty feet ahead and slipping from sight. Toro waved and shouted something that was muffled by the wind. His laughter carried much better.

"We will meet again soon," Ki said, feeling the bite of the storm, "and the results will be different. I pledge that to you, bullfighter."

Their coach quickly slowed as Ki climbed nimbly up on the coach's rooftop. The emergency hand brake was a small, spoked wheel. When his hands gripped it, they immediately froze to the metal. Ki tried to brace himself on the icy roof and gain some leverage. He felt the car come to a gentle halt, then begin to slip backward down the mountainside. The hand brake was frozen. The coach and caboose began to roll backward. Ki gritted his teeth and put all the strength of his body into his arms. He had to stop this train or it would begin to gather so much speed it would soon jump a curve and crash.

"Ahhhh!" he cried, striving with every fiber of his body until, finally, the hand brake yielded and began to turn. The flesh on the insides of his hands was torn away as Ki began to turn the wheel faster and faster. Down on the platform, he could hear Mark shouting, but there was no time to answer. The storm broke for an instant and Ki saw that they were gathering momentum with frightening suddenness. There was a curve less than half a mile down the track—a curve they could not possibly make. And even if the coach held to the track,

144

what then? A slow, lingering death by freezing?

One thing at a time, Ki told himself. First get this thing stopped, then think about survival. After that he would think about overtaking Toro Montoya and rescuing Jessie. And finally, he would help her to reclaim their Nevada mustangs.

# Chapter 13

Toro Montoya was the first one to retrace his way back across the long succession of cattle cars. He had almost lost his balance on the icy roofs a number of times and one of his men had plummeted to certain death. Now, as he forced his half-frozen body to navigate the icy ladder, he tried to think of what he could possibly say to Jessica Starbuck. Toro had no doubt that Ki had warned her of his movement to the rear car and, when he and Mark Lyon did not reappear, that she would know he was her enemy.

She would never believe him no matter how skillfully he lied to her, Toro thought. And anyway, when the storm cleared she would be able to see that the mail car and the caboose were missing. He had to find a way to control her until they reached Mexico. After that . . . well, perhaps by then he would be the master of her heart.

Toro landed on the platform, his legs so numb they felt like wooden stumps. He grabbed for the door, knowing his men were right behind him and that, rather than remain outside a moment longer than was necessary, they would trample him to death in their eagerness for shelter and warmth.

He threw the door open and, because his eyes were swimming with tears from the wind and cold, he stumbled completely into the coach before he saw Jessie standing in the aisle. He had to blink and wipe his eyes clear before he saw that there was a gun in her fist and a very determined look on her face.

"What happened to them?" she asked in a voice that was anything but trusting.

Toro heard heavy boots landing on the outside platform and then the man behind him staggered inside, half frozen.

"Take their guns as they come through the door and pitch them on the floor," Jessie ordered. "Do it slowly or so help me, I will kill you."

Toro tried to smile but his face was so numb he felt foolish, and his lips cracked so that he tasted blood. He was covered with snow and ice and there was no chance at all that he could charm this woman into being careless. With that decision, he did what she asked. It was simple because each of his men was half snow-blind. By the time he was finished, he had four men unarmed, and that was the last of them except for those he had ordered to await their arrival in Denver.

"On the floor, all of you!" Jessie ordered.

Toro sat down, almost falling because his feet and legs were still numb. The barrel of her gun remained pointed at Toro's heart.

"Are they dead?"

Toro was now very sure that he would have been a dead man himself if he had allowed his men to kill Ki and Mark or throw them from the train. "No," he said truthfully, "they are not."

Jessie studied the man, realizing that Toro was such a smooth-talking liar that she could not believe him. He would say anything to stay alive. "Where are they?"

"In the baggage car. We robbed it, Jessica."

"I can see the mail sacks. I don't give a damn about the money right now, I want Ki and Mark released safely."

"After we are set free with the money and the mustangs."

"Then Ki was right, you do work for Armando Escobar and the revolutionaries."

"I am sorry," he said with a shrug of his fine shoulders. "If he and his revolutionaries win, Señor Escobar has promised me the great bullfighting ring in Mexico City. It will become my stage, my reason for existence. Just as you will if you—"

Jessie cocked the gun but Toro did not flinch nor did his face betray any hint of fear. She had to admire his great courage, but she had heard enough lies. "Send a man back to release them or I will put bullets through both of your kneecaps so that you can never fight bulls again."

Now his face gave evidence of his fear, as Jessie had suspected it might. Toro Montoya, if that was his real name, was a bullfighter, she was certain of it. And one with immense pride, who would rather die than be unable to be the master of his bullring.

"By the Blessed Virgin herself," he breathed, "I can't bring your friends back. We uncoupled their coach."

Jessie tightened up inside and her finger squeezed the trigger. A bullet exploded in the coach and plucked at Toro's trouser leg. The man recoiled, but his voice somehow remained steady. "We could have killed them, but we did not. They are alive."

"But for how long? They will freeze to death before help arrives."

"No," he said. "There was a stove in the coach and wood to fuel it. If they run out, they can burn the big mail sacks or even the furniture inside. They will not freeze, Jessica. Nor starve. Ki will see to that."

The barrel of her gun moved a fraction off target. If he really had left them alive in the coach, they would survive. Ki would find a way to wait out help from the next train going east.

Jessie took a deep breath. "When we reach the first town, you will all be turned over to the sheriff as train robbers."

"I'm sorry," Toro said, "but that will not be the case."

"Give me one good reason why not. I'm the one holding a gun."

"But so is my man standing in the doorway behind you," Toro said, eyes flicking past her.

Jessie did not move a muscle. "You're bluffing."

"No," he said almost matter-of-factly, "I am not."

"Better believe him, Miss Starbuck," a voice said behind her. "I sure would hate to kill a woman as beautiful as you."

Jessie stiffened. Her father had once told her that life was like an all-night poker game and that too often you were dealt a bad hand. When that happened, you had to know when to fold or run a bluff. Bluffing was out of the question in this case; Toro had seen her cards and he was holding all the aces. Her daddy would have folded and waited for the next hand of cards. Jessie guessed she had better do the same.

"All right," she said, so angry she could have bitten nails in half. "You win."

"I always do," Toro said, finally breaking into that huge smile of his that she had once found so appealing but now infuriated her. "Especially in love."

"Not anymore," Jessie said coldly. "You will never make yourself a worse enemy than I am."

The smile died on his lips. Looking at him, Jessie was surprised to see that he was genuinely saddened. She did not care. He was her enemy and the enemy of the President of Mexico. Ki and Mark were no longer in a position to help her. She was on her own, and somehow, she was going to have to figure out a way to stop Toro and these men.

The temperature in Cheyenne was near to freezing when the train rolled into the station just after daybreak. Jessie had been kept under constant guard by Toro. Their trip since clearing the Wasatch Mountains had been uneventful. The train had pushed through Echo Canyon and into Wyoming. By the time they had reached Rock Springs, the weather had cleared and it had been smooth sailing across the high plains into Cheyenne.

Jessie had not had a moment's opportunity for escape, but as she felt the train slow going into Cheyenne she believed that her waiting was over. They would have to disembark this train and board another line that branched south to Denver. There might very well be several days between connections and Jessie thought she might find a way to escape. Not only that, but the six carloads of mustangs would also have to be unloaded and rerouted. Even with all of his men, Toro would be hard-pressed to be on guard every single moment.

Cheyenne shivered under a weak sun. Jessie stared out the window at a leaden sky and saw that the people standing on the railroad-station platform were heavily dressed and that when they spoke, steam came from their mouths. The temperature was in the midforties. She wondered how the mustangs had fared since she had seen them last in Utah. Toro and his men had worked hard at every stop to feed and water them, but there was little doubt that some had caught pneumonia. Jessie hated to even think of what shape the mustangs would be in by the time they reached Mexico. She could not help but wonder if they would be delivered by Toro to his revolutionaries, or to President González's soldiers as intended. Either way, the mustangs would need to be rested and fattened for several months before they would be fit enough for the cavalryman's saddle.

The train came to a full stop. Jessie saw the conductor stride along the station platform and, almost immediately, the boom on the water tower was lowered so that the train could take on more water for its boilers. Passengers began to disembark and when the train was almost empty. Toro nodded to his men.

They formed a human barrier both in front of and behind Jessie and Toro as they climbed stiffly out of their seats and began to move down the aisle. Toro took Jessie's arm and, when she pulled it roughly away, he said, "If you make a scene, I promise you, innocent people are going to die. Are a thousand mustangs worth even one person's life, Jessica?"

She looked into his face, damning him for his logic and intelligence. "No," she reluctantly conceded, "but I insist on seeing the mustangs and making sure they are properly fed and watered."

"All right," he said after a long pause. "But understand this. If you create trouble, I will not be able to control my men. Armando Escobar had promised them a bonus for delivery of these horses. They will not be denied."

When they stepped outside, the cold bite of fresh air sharpened Jessie's mind. She walked beside Toro looking neither right nor left but straight ahead, and her step was purposeful as she headed down the line toward the cattle cars filled with her mustangs. The Union Pacific stockmen were already moving the loading ramps up the side doors of the cattle cars. When the doors were pulled open, the mustangs stood packed end to end, heads down, bones protruding sharply against their shaggy coats.

Jessie bit her lip painfully. The mustangs looked half dead. They were so weak that they seemed to be holding each other erect and were unwilling or unable to take a single step toward the ramp.

A railroad stocktender jumped up on the ramp and began using a whip on the pathetically weak mustangs. Jessie broke free from Toro's arm and lunged through the fence rails to grab the man's upraised arm. Caught by surprise and momentarily overwhelmed by her savage fury, the man almost lost his balance and toppled to the track. But he recovered and reared back to strike Jessie in anger.

Toro's hand streaked for his gun and his bullet sent a neat hole through the palm of the stockman's hand. The man screamed in pain and the whip fell forgotten from his grasp.

"Get him out of here," Toro hissed at the men around him, "and get those mustangs down into the pen if you have to carry them!"

Jessie helped. Together, they began to lead the staggering horses down the ramp into the pens, where fresh water and hay awaited. Some of the mares were so weak they had to be slid down the ramps on their sides and then pulled into the stock pens and lifted to their feet.

"I want the best hay that money can buy, and grain, lots of grain," Jessie demanded.

"Are you buying?" Toro asked, "because I do not have unlimited funds."

"What good are dead horses—to either of us?"

"Then you still believe you can deliver them to González's soldiers," Toro said. "If that is true, then you and I, we should split the costs equally."

Jessie nodded. "Agreed. But you must also agree that these horses are in no shape to continue on without at least a week's rest here in Cheyenne. If we go sooner, all we will have is six boxcars of horsemeat."

Toro studied the animals as they were being unloaded. He shook his head with pity. "I cannot remain in Cheyenne that long. There is the matter of your friends to consider."

"Get the train schedules," Jessie said, no longer concerned about anything except the health of these half-starved mustangs. "It will tell you the soonest that Ki and Mark Lyon could catch the next train east and arrive here."

"I will do that," Toro said. "But you must also give

me your word that you will not try to escape."

"No."

"Then I will have the horses reloaded on the first train south to Denver," he said with finality.

"There is one going out first thing tomorrow morning," one of Toro's men said. "I'm from these parts and I've ridden it often. They come through here every three days."

Toro's face was uncompromising. "It is up to you, Jessica. Your word of honor that there will be no escape will buy these mustangs a few extra days of rest and feed. How do you decide?"

Jessie ground her teeth in anger and frustration. So far, Toro had played every card perfectly. But they were still almost seven hundred miles from the Mexican border and a lot could happen. Alex Starbuck had always said that, sooner or later, the luck of the cards was bound to change. Jessie figured her good luck was long overdue.

When the mustangs were reloaded at Cheyenne, their condition had visibly improved. That was what Jessie most admired about wild horses—they could take an enormous amount of physical abuse and yet recover with remarkable swiftness. They were, above all else, survivors.

The trip down to Denver was quick and there was no possibility of escape. Jessie knew that her time was running out like sand from an hourglass. She was determined to gain her own freedom. It would be a serious mistake to expect that Ki and Mark would be able to escape their snowbound baggage coach in northeastern Utah in time to be of help.

"We will stop for how long in Denver?" she asked, careful to keep the hope from creeping into her voice.

"Only one night," Toro said. "The mustangs will be unloaded, fed, and watered. The train south leaves tomorrow at noon. By that time, we will have the other half of the mustangs loaded. We'll freight them down to Deming, New Mexico, then drive them on horseback to the Mexican border."

"You could let me go south of Denver."

"And have you reach the nearest telegraph office and contact the U.S. marshal and his deputies in El Paso? No, thanks. I'm afraid that you're going all the way to Mexico, Jessica. After that, I will personally see that you are returned safely to Texas."

"You have everything planned out, don't you?"

"Yes. What else was there to do while you and your friends were mustanging?"

The train came to a stop in Denver. "I don't have to repeat all over again what would happen if you cried out for help or tried to escape, do I?" Toro asked, rising from his seat.

"No. I'll behave."

Toro chuckled. "Please, don't try to lull me into being careless. You are too much of a woman ever to give up so easily. I know that you would kill me the first time you had the opportunity. I wish I could trust you, but I can't."

One of the train robbers pointed out the window to a very lovely young woman. "Toro, look, it's Carmen! She sees you and is waving."

Toro had not been expecting to see Carmen again. Under the circumstances, he had regrettably decided that she would be an unsatisfactory complication and one that he did not need on top of all the other problems he now faced.

Jessie sensed his discomfort and she raised up in her seat a little and smiled down at the very beautiful woman. "Toro," she said, taking a hold of this unexpected opportunity, "don't you think you had better wave back to her?"

Toro waved, but now Carmen was staring at Jessie and her greeting had fizzled.

"Uh-oh," Jessie said, "how are you going to handle this situation, Don Juan?"

Toro smiled weakly. "I am not sure. Come on, let's go get this over with."

As they moved down the aisle, Jessie felt a surge of hope. Up till now, she had been insulated from everyone by Toro and his men. Under the threat of getting innocent passengers killed, she had been powerless to escape. But Carmen was the first crack to appear in Toro's otherwise flawless plans. Jessie meant to exploit the beautiful woman's arrival in any way she could.

By the time they met on the stage platform, Carmen's happiness had been displaced by seething anger. She was a beautiful but hot-tempered woman and Jessie did not mind being the object of her jealous wrath.

"Who is this on your arm, Toro!" she yelled loud enough to turn the heads of passersby. "I come to surprise you and I find you with this . . . this woman!"

Toro grabbed her by one arm, and with Jessie on the other, he half dragged the protesting Carmen away from the crowd.

"Let go of me!" Carmen shouted. "You said that you would take me with you to Mexico! That I would throw you roses in the bullring and you would return kisses! And now . . . now I find you in the arms of another woman!" She was almost hysterical.

"Carmen, please! I was coming to get you. I swear it."

"No, you only wanted the damned horses!"

"That's not true. And this woman, she is—"

"I love you!" Carmen wailed. She grabbed Toro and squeezed his neck until his face reddened. Her eyes raked those of Jessie. "This! This is my man! Try to take him from me and I will fight you!"

Jessie nodded agreeably. "He is yours completely, Carmen. Ask him to let me walk away and I will not even look back."

Carmen blinked. "You mean this?"

"Yes."

"Then let her go, Toro!"

He had to clear his voice several times, for she had almost crushed his throat. "I can't, my love. This is the woman I told you about. This is Miss Jessica Starbuck. It is her mustangs that we have taken. If I let her go, then she will summon the American authorities and we will all go to prison."

Carmen finally understood the situation. "Oh, well, why didn't you say so!" She pushed out her hand. "I have heard so much about you, Miss Starbuck. It is a pleasure."

Jessie took her hand and shook it. She had never met anyone quite like Carmen. The woman was crazy about Toro, and fiercely possessive as well. Jessie hugged Toro's arm and smiled up into his face with benign radiance. It was get-even time. "Toro, my dear, this must be the lovely woman you told me about. The one that fathered you a son in Mexico City?"

Carmen's hand turned to ice. Her voice had the sound of breaking glass. "He told you he had a woman in Mexico City?"

"She is lying!" Toro shouted, pushing Jessie into the arms of one of his men. "Carmen, my love, don't you see that she is trying to drive a wedge between us?"

"And she has succeeded! You said nothing about fathering a son."

Toro grabbed her and wrestled her behind a baggage car. Jessie shook free of the man who held her and, hands on hips, she listened with satisfaction to the raging argument.

"Lady," the man said beside her, "it's pretty plain to see what your game is, but it's a dangerous one. You cause too much hell and I'll kill you the first time Toro isn't looking. I'll personally heave your body out the moving train for the coyotes to eat."

Jessie's smile vanished, but she said nothing. Still,

she took comfort in the fact that she had planted the first seed of doubt in Carmen's mind, and the woman was not about to remain behind in Denver. Toro was a liar. She had no sympathy for him whatsoever and she knew that he had not intended to bring Carmen along to Mexico.

For the first time in a week, Jessie began to feel real hope. Carmen's explosive jealousy was the key to Toro's downfall. Jessie could now see that very clearly. But the man beside her was not bluffing. If she was not very, very careful, she would end up facedown alongside the railroad tracks somewhere in southern New Mexico.

Ki, she thought, wistfully, what I wouldn't give for your help now.

# Chapter 14

Ki stood on the platform of the eastbound Union Pacific train and pitched coal into the firebox. It was freezing cold here in central Wyoming, but he did not feel anything except the fierce heat. He and Mark had commandeered this locomotive in the Wasatch Mountains and Ki was still shoveling coal with a relentless intensity three hundred miles later.

"You're not human, you're an engine!" Mark yelled into the wind. "It isn't normal the way you been shoveling coal. Let's trade places."

Ki shook his head vigorously. His face was shiny with sweat and his palms were blistered, but he found this activity to his liking after having spent almost a full week inside the stranded mail coach. They had all suffered, especially Mark, who had no patience and had blamed himself for the fact that Jessie had been kidnapped by Toro and his train robbers.

Ki knew that to rage helplessly was a waste of mental energy. He had fashioned a pair of snowshoes from the bark and thin branches of trees. In the time that followed, he had also made a crude but very powerful bow and two arrows, which he had used to hunt. He had tracked an eight-point buck for sixteen hours before he had killed it and that meat had fed them all until help had arrived.

Remaining near the snowbound coach had been one of the most difficult times of Ki's life. Every hour that he had spent waiting for help had been a personal agony. He had slept little. His unusually disciplined mind had almost rioted with thoughts that Jessie might be killed by Toro's men. Had he not sincerely believed that the handsome Spaniard was not a cold-blooded murderer, he would have abandoned the weak and wounded and struck out on his snowshoes across the Continental Divide toward New Mexico. But having been deprived of firearms by the train robbers, Mark and those wounded left behind might very well have starved before another train came by to help.

When it did come, it was sheer good fortune. Luck brought them a locomotive pushing an immense iron snowplow. It had been clearing the tracks in anticipation of the first train that would come through the Wasatch Mountains after the big snowstorm. The locomotive engineer had been amazed to discover their tracks were blocked by a caboose and mail coach. He had argued fiercely to hook it up and pull it back down to Salt Lake. But Ki and Mark had taken command and forced the engineer to knock the two cars off the tracks with their wedge-shaped snowplow. At gunpoint, Mark had made the engineer show him how to operate the locomotive and then Ki had taken over the fireman's job of feeding the coal to the firebox.

Secure in the knowledge that a passenger train out of Salt Lake City would soon be along, they blasted over the mountains and into Wyoming. Through isolated towns they traveled, pulling only the single coal car, and their speed had never been equaled across the empty, frigid land. The buffalo were gone, but bands of antelope scattered at their passing and an occasional cowboy riding the snow-blanketed range would pull off his hat and wave it to the sky.

"Is that Cheyenne?" Mark called late that night.

Ki straightened and leaned out into the biting wind to see a collection of lights winking out of the darkness.

"Yes," he said. "We'll have to do some fast talking to switch to the branch line south."

"You leave that to me," Mark said. "Try and find us some food to eat. We'll be leaving within an hour."

Ki almost fell from the car, he was so weary. It would have been fine to just sit and rest, but he knew that he was too hot to do that in this cold weather, and that sudden inactivity could bring on pneumonia if his body cooled down too fast. So he struck out for the heart of town, looking for a late-night cafe where he could buy food.

He found everything all locked up, except for one cafe where a man was cleaning up inside. He battered on the door until he received attention.

"What the hell do you want, Chinaman?" a fat, greasy-looking man wearing a dirty apron demanded as he opened the door a crack.

"Food," Ki said. "I have money." He dug out a wad of bills.

"Dammit, we are closed for the night! Can't you read the sign, dumb—"

Ki was not in an especially tolerant mood. His hand came up and before the cook could react, Ki's thumb was digging for an *atemi* pressure point near the base of the cook's thick neck.

"Hey, what—"

He sagged into unconsciousness and Ki dragged him inside and closed the door. He moved to the pantry and found a loaf of bread, a pound of good cheese, and a huge bologna wrapped in butcher's brown paper. There was a quart of fresh milk in a pitcher beside the cupboard and Ki drained it with relish, then grabbed a bag and stuffed everything inside, including a fresh apple pie.

"Have a good night's sleep," he said, stepping over the cook and dropping a dollar on his chest before heading out the door.

When he returned to the locomotive, he discovered that Mark had also been forced to resort to physical measures with the stationmaster. The man was howling in protest through a gag, and there was a nasty bruise on his cheek, in addition to one eye which was rapidly swelling shut. When he saw Ki he howled even louder, but he continued to finish switching the tracks so that their snowplow locomotive was heading south toward Denver.

"How long ago since Toro and the mustangs came through here?" Ki asked.

Mark blinked. "Damn! I been so busy with this bull-headed fella, I forgot to ask."

Ki yanked the gag from the stationmaster's mouth. "How long?" he demanded.

"Two and a half days, but I swear you ain't leavin' this—"

Ki jammed the gag back inside the man's mouth. "We had better take him for a ride to Denver, Mark. If he stays here we'll have a welcoming party when we arrive, and we haven't time to go before a judge and explain everything."

Mark nodded. "I agree. In fact, I'm not sure we could explain our way out of jail. We've stolen a loco-motive, Ki. It must be worth five thousand dollars, at least."

The stationmaster was raging so hard his face was purple. Ki pulled out the gag once more, afraid the man might be choking to death. "Twelve thousand!" he shouted. "This train and coal car are worth at least twelve thousand and you'll both go to—"

Ki stuffed the gag back inside and then shoved the man up into the locomotive. Mark had not shut down the boiler, but the steam pressure had died a little while Ki was gone, so he began shoveling in more coal. While the pressure built to operating speed, they de-voured the bread, bologna, and apple pie.

Mark took a deep breath and licked his lips clean. "Nothing like a feast to pick a man up again, is there?"

In answer, Ki grabbed the shovel and set to work until the fire was raging. He felt Mark release the steam that powered the driving wheels, and then the locomotive was gathering momentum out of Cheyenne. Five miles south, they were hurtling through the night at a speed that left the stationmaster paralyzed with fear.

*Two and a half days' headstart,* Ki thought as he shoveled like a man possessed. *Toro will not expect us to be that close behind him, but then, he is not a fool willing to take chances. He will try to leave Denver immediately.*

Ki took a deep breath. Even if Toro and his men had already departed Denver with Jessie and the one thousand mustangs, nothing was changed. *I will hunt them down if I have to go all the way to Mexico City,* Ki thought. And if any harm has come to Jessie, I will kill every man responsible.

Ki began to sweat again. The blisters on his hands reopened, and yet he continued to shovel like a man possessed. He had fed this engine all the way across Wyoming. Feeding it down to New Mexico was equally within his power.

Jessie watched as the mustangs were reloaded from he Denver stock pens. The first batch they had captured and sent ahead were already in good flesh. She was thankful to Carmen who, she learned, had been responsible for their care and feeding. The second bunch were stronger than they had been in Cheyenne, but not much. They had lost about twenty to sickness and infirmity. Considering what the animals had been through, that was very good. Jessie was certain that many more wild horses would have died on the range if she and Three Kills' Indians had not captured them.

Jessie thought about the Paiute chief. Both she and

162

Mark had promised that they would move mountains, if necessary, to help those Nevada Indians own their land. But if she were killed trying to escape, could Mark keep that promise? Jessie hoped so. She also recalled how she had ordered her men to deliver five thousand head of Circle Star cattle to the poor people of Mexico. She wondered if they had been delivered on time and wished she could have seen the faces of the *peones* who received them. Ed Wright had been told to give the *peones* some of her best Circle Star cows, heifers, and young bulls so that their pure blood might be used to upgrade that of the generally inferior Mexican cattle.

When Jessie thought of all that she had done and intended to do yet, it gave her hope and fresh purpose. Never before had she been tricked and then rendered helpless. Toro used every bit of leverage he had at his disposal when he warned her that an attempted escape would surely result in innocent deaths.

But there ought to be dozens of stops between here and the end of the line where she could escape and wire ahead to the authorities in El Paso. This entire mustanging operation was supposed to be carried out secretively, but that might not be possible any longer. Jessie had no doubt that the United States President would rather have it known he sympathized with his counterpart in Mexico than have the mustangs fall into the hands of the revolutionaries. Especially since their leader, Armando Escobar, had vowed to attack and regain Texas.

Their train pulled out of Denver without incident, although the sight of eleven cattle cars filled with mustangs did cause quite a stir and not a few questions. Toro handled all inquiries smoothly, stating that the animals were for various military outposts in the Southwest and that he was an Army horse buyer. Jessie watched him charm a young Denver newspaper reporter with his slick story. She could not help but marvel at Toro's smoothness. *The man should have been a politician instead of a bullfighter. He has missed his calling,* she thought.

Beside her in the aisle seat, Carmen said, "You watch him very closely. Are you in love with my Toro?"

Jessie shook her head. "I admire him in some ways. He is also a very handsome man."

"And a brave one, Miss Starbuck."

"Yes, I know that. But not an especially faithful one."

If Jessie expected her to flare up with anger, she was in for a surprise. Carmen's eyes reflected pain, not anger. "When one loves such a man so strongly, one is a fool. I know that."

"And you can live with it?"

"For maybe ten or fifteen years while his juices are hot, sure. But when he gets older, perhaps he will slow down a little. When he cannot fight the bulls any longer, maybe he will see that other things are more important. Like a family. A loving wife who knows the meaning of forgiveness."

Jessie shook her head. "He is a very lucky man to have someone as understanding as you."

"I know," Carmen said. She leaned closer. The sound of the train whistle and the noise of departure made hearing difficult and she did not want a guard to overhear her next words. "I also know that some of Toro's men have decided it is best to kill you before we cross the border."

Jessie's lovely face did not reflect her thoughts. She had already guessed as much. If she were seen and her death were traced to Toro and the revolutionaries, it would cause great repercussions that would reach all the way to the President's office. Alex Starbuck had collected many IOU's in his long and brilliant financial career, and they were still collectible in this nation's highest centers of power.

Carmen continued. "I think, if you were murdered, that Toro would never live to see the bullring in Mexico

City. They would take the horses but have to kill him. Your name and the good things you have already done for Mexico would make this necessary."

"You are very bright and perceptive, Carmen. So what have you decided?"

"To help you escape," she whispered.

"When?" Jessie could feel her heart beating faster. If she could talk this woman into helping her get free soon enough . . .

"At the border," Carmen said.

"I will probably be dead by then."

Carmen closed her eyes and leaned her head back against the seat. "You are right," she confessed. "That would be too late. I will help you sooner."

"How soon?"

"I don't know, Miss Starbuck. If we are caught in the attempt, they will kill both of us. We must think and watch together."

Jessie nodded. She saw Toro shake the newspaper reporter's hand and then move briskly toward the coach. The train jerked forward and the whistle blew with shrill urgency. It was telling Jessie that half of her hourglass of time had spilled out. She knew that, somehow, she must escape within the next four or five hundred miles or she was a dead woman.

Her chance came a day later when the train was caught in a sudden blizzard thirty miles south of Raton Pass, where some snow-blind cattle had drifted across the tracks. The brakes had been applied, but even so the cowcatcher had still struck the milling herd and killed several of the beasts. When the train had stopped, many of the more uneducated passengers had thought that the train might have hit an elk or possibly even a buffalo herd. They had grabbed their rifles and jumped down to the roadbed and hurried forward. Toro had gone ahead too, furious at the delay. The guard he had left behind

165

looked bored and Jessie knew he had been drinking from a hip flask.

It was time. She looked at Carmen and then pointed at the guard. The woman understood. She arose from her seat and went over to strike up a conversation. Jessie slipped out of her seat, but the guard caught her movement.

"Hey!" he said, suddenly forgetting about Carmen. "Where the hell do you think you're going!"

"To the ladies' room," she said coldly.

"I better go along and stand by the door or Toro will—"

"I have to go, too. Let me watch her," Carmen said.

"Uh, I dunno."

Carmen smiled innocently. "I am not to be trusted?"

The guard stammered, "I didn't mean that! It's just that Miss Starbuck is known as a woman who can handle guns."

"So am I," Carmen said with pouting lips, taking his sixgun and aiming it at Jessie. "And if she tries anything, it would be a great pleasure to kill her!"

The man smiled knowingly. He had it all figured out. Toro had two jealous women. "Ah, hell, go ahead. Just be careful is all."

They walked down the aisle, moving as quickly as possible. The ladies' room was in the next coach, but they stopped when they were outside on the platform. "Thanks," Jessie said. "But how will you explain this?"

"I will take Toro to bed and explain everything," Carmen said with a wink. "Besides, he does not want you killed either. Only his men do. Take this gun and go quickly. A few minutes after the train begins to move, I will run back to tell the guard that you have escaped."

Jessie took the gun and shoved it into her pocket. The snow was blowing hard and it was freezing cold. She wished she had thought of a way to take her coat, but that would have been obvious even to the stupid guard.

"I won't forget you," she said.

"Just promise me this. If we don't reach Mexico, then you must help me save Toro from prison. It would kill a man of his spirit to be locked up behind bars."

"I can't promise you anything."

"He is the only reason why you are still alive," Carmen said stubbornly.

"And the reason why I have been a hostage. I'm sorry."

"It does not change anything. I have done many bad things, but never have I been part of a murder. I did not want your death to put a stain on my eternal soul." She crossed herself.

Jessie understood. Like many Catholic women, Carmen had a very strong moral upbringing that drew a line which could not be crossed. She might commit many sins of the flesh, but not the sin of murder.

She left Carmen as the train whistle blew, urging the passengers to get aboard before they were left behind in this snowy wilderness. Jessie glanced to both sides of the train and, to her horror, she realized that they were on open ground and that there was no place to hide. She did the only thing she could—rolled underneath the train and hugged the crossties.

She could feel the train begin to move, feel the roadbed groan with the weight of the rolling stock. Terror gripped her and she wondered if anything hung low enought to crush her as it passed overhead. The wheels were churning and clanging as they began to revolve faster and faster.

Suddenly, she felt something pluck at her hair and she lifted her fingers until she touched passing steel. In this manner, she gauged the distance she could raise her head. Something bit into her forearm. She felt warm blood trickle down her arm and knew that she could not have been struck by an object hanging from the undercarriage of the train or it would have first struck her fingers. Jessie dared to raise her head and turn it. When she did, she saw two of Toro's men standing at the edge of the railroad bed, firing between the passing wheels at her!

The answer was clear. Carmen had mistakenly spread the alarm a few minutes too soon. Soon enough for Toro's men to jump back down to the roadbed and search for her under the train. Jessie flattened, but when another bullet seared across her shoulder blades, she lifted her head again and managed to get the sixgun pointed at the men. This was crazy! She had to fire between the wheels, which were passing in ever-shorter intervals. Jessie took aim, waited for a clear shot, and then took it. Her first bullet brought one of the men down, clutching a hole in his chest. The second man, realizing he was either going to die or be left abandoned in a blizzard, gave up the hunt and disappeared with a leaping dive back onto the platform.

Jessie's gun sagged and she hugged the crossties again. She caught the scent of the mustangs as they passed overhead, and then two more cars swept by. Suddenly, as the thundering noise diminished, she felt the falling snow on her cheek. A few minutes later the roadbed stopped shivering and there was a terrible silence.

Jessie sat up and looked around. She was free, but it was going to be a long, cold walk back to Raton Pass. She climbed shakily to her feet and started moving. If she could get to a telegraph operator before Toro thought to order the lines cut, maybe there was a chance she could have the train stopped in time.

# Chapter 15

Jessie wondered if she was going to freeze to death before she reached help. Her left forearm no longer ached where the train robber's bullet had grazed her, but instead had grown numb from the cold. She knew that Raton Pass was somewhere up ahead, and yet the snow was becoming deeper and her strength was starting to ebb.

Suddenly she felt a faint vibration on the tracks, and then, as she stood dazed and swaying with fatigue, a locomotive thundered out of the curtain of whiteness. Jessie yelled and threw herself sideways as the snow-plow-clad locomotive roared past. She rolled and then tried to raise her head, but the locomotive had vanished into the blizzard.

Jessie wiped the snow from her face and bit her lips to hide her crushing disappointment. If she had only know that a train would be coming! She hung her head and tried to gather her strength to continue on.

After several long minutes, the faint but unmistakable sound of a locomotive's whistle cut through the wind and storm. It sounded like it was coming across a hundred miles of mountaintops. Jessie crawled back to the track, then knelt beside the narrow-gauge rails, feeling their shiver grow stronger, hearing the locomotive's whistle growing louder by the second. A tight grin formed on her bloodless lips and she pushed herself to her feet. The locomotive engineer or his fireman had seen her and they were coming back!

The rear of the coal car butted out of the falling snow like a tug punching through coastal fog, then Ki was yelling and dropping down to the roadbed. "Jessie!" he shouted, moving toward her, his smile wider than she had ever seen it before.

She laughed, threw herself into his arms, and gave him a big hug. "Ki, you've no idea how good it is to see you again. What happened to Mark, did he—"

"No," Ki said. "He's the one operating the locomotive! I'm just the fireman shoveling coal."

Jessie stepped back. Ki's face was streaked with sweat and coal dust. She looked at his hands and saw how badly they had been used. "You've got yourself a helper now."

Ki's smile died. "I can't let you shovel coal."

"Who said anything about shoveling? I'll have Mark teach me how to run that locomotive. I've always wanted to try. *He* can shovel for a while!"

Ki laughed, took her hand in his own, and led her forward. "You're freezing, aren't you?"

"Who wouldn't be in this weather?"

Ki helped her up into the cab of the locomotive, where Mark grabbed her and gave her a welcoming hug. The fire was roaring in the firebox and the heat felt wonderful.

"How far behind are we?" Ki asked.

"About six hours. Did you think to telegraph the El Paso authorities yet?"

"Yes," Ki answered. "We stopped in Raton Pass, but Toro had already had the lines leading south cut."

"Then we'll just have to catch him," Jessie said, studying the steam gauges and levers before her. "Mark, if you'll show me what to do, then grab that extra coal shovel, I think we can really make this bucket of tin fly!"

Ki and Mark exchanged surprised glances.

"Did I say something wrong?" Jessie asked.

"No," Mark said, "but we've already been highballing it all the way through Wyoming and Colorado. The way Ki has been shoveling coal, I'm surprised we haven't burned out the engine."

Jessie unwrapped a woolen scarf from around her neck, then tore it in half. She carefully wrapped Ki's blistered hands. "With you both shoveling, we ought to almost double the speed. We're going to catch Toro and those mustangs before they reach those Mexican revolutionaries, even if we have risk blowing this engine to pieces."

Mark grabbed a shovel and drove it into the dwindling supply of coal. "I just hope there's enough of this stuff to get us to Deming."

"If there isn't," Ki said, "we'll feed it some forest. There is nothing that can stop us now."

Jessie agreed. With Ki and Mark's help, she knew that her luck had finally changed for the better. Never mind that they would be badly outgunned when they overtook Toro and his men. They would find a way to win and regain those mustangs for the President of Mexico. That had been another of Alex Starbuck's rules—winners always won when the stakes were their lives and fortunes.


"There it is!" Jessie cried, hand on the throttle. "We've caught them!"

Ki and Mark leaned out over the tracks. They could see the train about a mile up ahead and, even though it was pulling a line of passenger and cattle cars, it was moving fast.

Ki frowned, then pitched in the last bit of coal before slamming the door shut. The steam gauges were holding steady, but they all knew that the pressure would soon begin to drop as the fire consumed the last of their precious coal.

"Give it all she has," Ki said grimly. "If we can touch the last cattle car with our snowplow, Mark and I can jump and make our way across the rooftops to the passenger cars."

"They'd be expecting that," Jessie shouted. "You wouldn't have a chance up there!"

"It's the only chance we have," Mark replied, eyes watching the steam-gauge needle as it began to quiver and then, very slowly and heartbreakingly, edge downward. "We have to try it!"

Jessie kept her hand on the throttle as the distance between them shrank. A half mile, then a quarter, and now she could even smell the packed cattle cars. They were flying through heavy forest. If they had been on a slight downgrade, she would have felt more confident that their greater momentum would have brought them up to bump the train ahead.

"Come on!" she cried, pushing the throttle hard, willing the engine to give more than it possessed. "Don't do this to us!"

But a steam locomotive doesn't care about anything except the fire in its belly, and this one was running on dying flames. They came to within a hundred yards of the train and then their speed fell to the point of no return. Jessie wanted to scream with frustration as the car filled with mustangs slowly began to edge away.

"Dammit!" Mark screamed in a choking voice as he and Ki stood watching helplessly with their useless shovels in hand.

Jessie bit back her own crushing disappointment. She looked at Ki, whose face was grim but filled with determination. Jessie saw a fallen tree near the line nearly half a mile up ahead. She began to apply the brakes. They would load that dead tree into the coal car piece by termite-infested piece. And if it was not enough to get them to the end of the line in Deming, then be damned, they'd find another tree!

172

The train ahead gave a triumphant parting blast that sounded very much like a laugh, and Jessie knew that Toro had ordered it to break their spirits.

Rotting pine wood could never fire as hot as coal, so their locomotive wasn't going to overtake Toro. But the finish line of this race wasn't Deming. Maybe it wasn't even the Mexican border thirty miles farther south. No, the finish line was wherever she, Mark, and Ki overtook Toro and the outlaw band. And the winner was whoever ended up with the Nevada mustangs.

The Atchison, Topeka & Santa Fe line fed into the Southern Pacific line, and that was where they found the empty cattle cars resting on a siding. Thirty miles south lay the Mexican border and the strife-torn state of Chihuahua. Jessie knew that was where they would find Toro Montoya, Armando Escobar, and all the revolutionaries. And if they were lucky, maybe they would also find President González's soldiers and some badly needed help. One thing she was certain of was that neither she nor her companions were going to let a small matter of long odds stop them now. Besides, they and the Paiutes had gone through hell and back to capture those mustangs and none of them knew the word "quitter."

So they bought the best horses money could buy, along with saddles, bedrolls, food, and supplies for the trail of their mustangs. And each of them bought a new Winchester rifle and a hundred rounds of ammunition. Toro's trail was as broad as the Rio Grande and just as easy to follow. Had it not been for the fact that the mustangs were so weak, Toro would probably have run the giant herd clear to the border.

"How far ahead are they?" Jessie asked.

"A day," Ki answered. "Maybe a few hours less."

"Then we'll ride all night and all tomorrow if need be."

"We'll be in Old Mexico by tomorrow morning," Mark observed, shading his eyes and looking out into the washed-out colors of the high desert.

Jessie shoved her new Winchester into its scabbard and pulled her hat low over her eyes. "Good thing we all speak a little Spanish," she said, touching the spurs to her horse as she galloped out of Deming.

★

# Chapter 16

Ki knelt in the soft sand of Mexico and examined the tracks. "They were joined here by a large number of horsemen, Jessie. Then they all went south toward those low mountains."

"But who?" she asked out loud. "Were they met by President González's forces, or those of the revolutionary, Armando Escobar? That's the question."

Ki swung into the saddle. It was about eleven in the morning and the tracks were only a few hours old. He did not like the fact that they were leading them into rough country where they might easily be ambushed, but they would have to take the risk and keep following.

"There is only one way to find out who they joined up with," Ki said.

Jessie nodded and they rode on.

It was late afternoon when Ki raised his hand and motioned for silence. Ahead of them the tracks disappeared into the mouth of a narrow canyon. Ki had seen nothing to indicate that this was a trap, but something instinctive told him that, if they rode into the mouth of the canyon, they would never live to pass through.

Dismounting, he indicated with hand motions for Jessie and Mark to ride the horses into a stand of mesquite where they would hidden from view. Then he ran to the base of the rocks and began to climb. The cliff was eighty feet high and steep, but he made it effortlessly. And when he neared the rim, he slipped over, staying low to the ground as he darted into a cover of rocks.

There were three Mexican revolutionaries sitting atop the cliff. They were talking softly, their eyes straying down to the lean strip of canyon floor below them. Ki could smell the tobacco they smoked. Occasionally, one laughed with a guttural sound.

He slipped two of his *shuriken* blades from out of his vest and stepped out from the rocks into clear view. They saw him at the same instant and their hands went for their guns as if the motion had been rehearsed.

Ki's hand was a blur of motion and the first of his *shuriken* blades buried itself in one man's throat. Before a bullet was fired, his second blade found another man's blood and sent him tumbling over the side of the cliff, voice trailing away like smoke.

The last man fired, but his panic was so great that his bullet went wide. Ki was on him in three bounds, and the hard edge of his hand caught the man in the throat and drove him to the earth. When the sentry cocked his gun to fire again, Ki sent a sweep-lotus kick to his face and the Mexican was flung over the edge of the cliff.

Five minutes later, Jessie, Ki, and Mark rode silently through the narrow defile and into a succession of great canyons that grew progressively greener, fed by a sparkling stream.

They stopped an hour later and all of them knew they had finally come to the last canyon, the place of the revolutionaries.

"We had better go ahead on foot. Try to scale the rocks and circle in from the far side," Jessie said.

Mark untied his rope and so did Ki. The walls of this canyon were much higher and would be far more difficult to scale. None of them liked the idea of leaving their horses, but they knew they would die if they attempted to ride into that trap.

Mark thumbed his hat back and stared up at the rim.

"Well," he drawled, "I was ready to fight off a hundred or so revolutionaries, but I sure hadn't planned on becoming a mountain goat!"

Jessie forced a grin. "We'll make it, all right. And when we get up there, it ought to be a very interesting sight."

Both men nodded. Ki selected the best point of attack and strode toward the rock face with all the confidence of a man who did this every day of his life. When he reached the base of the cliff, he put his hands and bare feet into a crevasse and began to climb rapidly. When he reached an outcropping of rocks about twenty feet above them, he stopped, tied his rope around his waist, and threw the end down for Jessie.

"Jesus," Mark whispered almost reverently, "being around him sure can make a man feel inferior!"

For the first time in his life, Toro Montoya was also feeling very inferior. Arms pulling almost out of his shoulder sockets, he dangled from the end of a rope and studied the scene before him. Every last one of his men had been hacked to death with machetes and now lay scattered around the camp exactly where they had fallen. Carmen was crouched in the dirt, her blouse ripped open to reveal her lovely bosom. There was a livid bruise on her cheek where she had been knocked momentarily senseless by the revolutionist; Armando Escobar had tried to fondle her breasts and received a hard slap for his crude behavior.

But worst of all, Toro felt his ankles being tied separately. Each rope led to the saddlehorn of a rider who would soon receive the order to back his horse and rip him apart between the legs if he did not tell this animal what he wanted to know.

"I did what you ordered!" he gasped. "I did what I was paid to do! The mustangs are yours now instead of belonging to the Presidente's soldiers. I have done all that was asked of me. Is this the way you repay success?"

Armando Escobar was young, too young to be a general. His face was round, his eyes deep-set under beetle brows. He was fifty pounds too heavy and his stomach hung over his ornate silver belt buckle like a bag of oats. There was a cruel cut to his mouth, and his mustache and beard were thin and scraggly. Of ordinary height, he wore specially designed boots that raised him to nearly six feet. His nose was flat and utterly cruel.

"I have been told," Escobar said in a voice that dripped with contempt, "that you had the opportunity to bring me much money. That you failed to take it from the Indians and that you released the rich young Señorita Starbuck. Is that success, Señor Montoya? No, it is treason!"

Carmen lifted her head. "It was I who released her!" she cried. "Not him. I let Miss Starbuck escape."

"You!" Escobar shouted. "You whore, you shall also die slowly and—"

"No," Toro grated. "She lies. I let Miss Starbuck go. Not her. Me! And I would do it again rather than have her fall into the hands of a pig like you!"

It worked. His insult so inflamed the revolutionary that Escobar attacked and used his fists to beat Toro's face and body. Toro felt himself losing consciousness. He prayed this man would beat him to death quickly instead of having the pleasure of using a very slow torture.

Jessie, Ki, and Mark watched and heard the scene below. Jessie felt cold anger flood her veins and she gripped her rifle, wishing she could put a bullet through Escobar's head. But she did not, because that would have been their own death sentence.

"He is out now," Ki said, when Toro's head dropped to his chest. "He feels nothing any longer."

"Did he tell that fat sonofabitch he let you go?" Mark

178

asked. "My Spanish is not too good."

"Yes," Jessie said, studying Toro's long body and remembering how they had made love. She no longer felt angry that she had given herself freely to that man. With his act of heroism, Toro had completely redeemed himself in her eyes. "He lied to save his woman. And I want to save him."

They both looked at her strangely.

"No," she whispered. "Not for myself. But because he deserves to live. He is not like them. He has been our enemy, but he does not deserve to die, and certainly not this way."

Ki nodded. "You'll want the girl, too."

"Yes."

"Oh, that's rich," Mark said, shaking his head in disbelief. "Down there we have a thousand mustangs and two hostages. And three of us—count us, one, two, three—are supposed to somehow save them all."

"No," Jessie said. "Not three. Two. You are going to find the President's soldiers and bring them running. It's our only hope."

Mark stared at them. "And leave you and Ki here to—hell, no!"

Ki started to say something, but Jessie silenced him with a look, then touched Mark's arm. "I wouldn't ask you to do this if it wasn't vital. You have the letter sent to your father by President González. We may die here, but if the President's soldiers come, they'd not only have their mustangs, but they would also capture the revolutionaries. Don't you see the stakes here? If you bring help, we cannot fail!"

Mark hated the idea of leaving them alone. Jessie could see the frustration and protest in his eyes, but also the knowledge that she was correct.

"All right," he said finally. "I'll go now. Don't do anything until I get back with help. I promise you I will be back soon!"

Jessie nodded and kissed him before turning back to stare down at the big camp below. Toro was unconscious and probably would be for a long time. But Carmen was being dragged screaming to her feet and Escobar was bellowing for tequila and music. He will get drunk to drown his pride and bring out the basest part of him, Jessie thought, and then after dark he will do unspeakable things to that poor woman.

"Ki, we must go down there as soon as it is dark."

"I know," he said, understanding her completely.

Jessie settled back to wait until nightfall. No question about it, going down into that camp before Mark returned with help was foolish. To save the life of Toro and the self-respect of Carmen, she was willing to risk everything—even their own lives. But not to do anything—that was to lose her own self-respect.

Jessie studied the valley and the scattered campfires below. One large tent dominated the camp, and that was where Escobar had just dragged Carmen, screaming and kicking.

"It is time to go."

Ki nodded. He had transformed himself into a *ninja*, an ancient sect of Japanese assassins trained in all the arts of killing by stealth. He had blackened his face and the back of his hands with a piece of charcoal. In Japan, the *ninja* were even feared by the samurai, because they were absolutely committed to their duty. *Ninja* were trained to kill without hesitation, using all the weapons known to their countrymen. Tonight, Jessie knew that Ki possessed only his *shuriken* and the short-bladed *tanto* knife. But his mind and body were equally dangerous.

They started down the cliff walls, Ki moving first, lowering himself on the linked ropes. When they both had reached their end, Ki somehow twisted on the line and the rope came untied from above. He caught it soundlessly and then found a thick piece of brush jutting out from the ledge to which they clung precariously. Ki tied the rope again and they continued on down until they reached the valley floor.

The camp was alive with laughter and conversation. There were at least a dozen women, probably whores paid to keep the men happy and occupied. Jessie and Ki had determined that there were only two guards, and these were located at the entrance to the canyon. Ki disappeared along the canyon wall where not even the light of moon or stars infiltrated the absolute darkness. Jessie heard nothing, but the *ninja* master returned a few minutes later and she knew the guards had died in quick silence.

They moved deeper into the canyon's end toward the horses. The nearly one thousand mustangs had been placed in a huge holding pen near the saddle horses. Jessie and Ki had no trouble selecting four animals for their escape and readying them with the great-horned Mexican saddles and Spanish bits.

Guitars began to play loudly and the music was punctuated by the sounds of clapping hands and hoots of laughter. Jessie and Ki led the horses away from the others into the shadows, where they were tied and left in waiting. She and Ki had discussed this before, and there had been some disagreement. Ki had very much wanted her to stay with the horses while he rescued Carmen and then attempted to steal across the open ground and free Toro from his bonds. Jessie had refused that plan. She would go with Ki to save Carmen and then return to the horses and await Ki and Toro's return.

Not twenty feet from the tent, Jessie heard Carmen's scream, but before she could jump forward, Ki took her arm and prevented her from revealing their presence. A moment passed and then they moved swiftly toward the rear of the tent. A faint illumination glowed through the canvas and Jessie knew it was from a single candle. She heard another scream and then Escobar's hurt and outraged cry of anger. Flesh slapped flesh and Ki's *tanto* blade was flashing through the canvas, parting it like torn newsprint. The *ninja* went through the slit in the canvas like a wraith and, even before Jessie could enter, she heard a sudden throat-rattle and knew that Armando Escobar was a dead man.

Carmen was on the cot, her clothes ripped, her face swollen and lips bleeding. When she saw Ki, she started to scream, but then Jessie appeared and she froze with indecision.

"Hush," Jessie whispered urgently as she took the woman's hand. "We are leaving now."

Carmen looked from one to the other of them and rose shakily to her feet. "What about Toro?" she said in a choked whisper. "We can't just leave him to be tortured to death. When they find this animal . . ."

Jessie followed her eyes to the dead revolutionary leader. There was not a mark on Escobar. No sign of blood or of struggle, but only a slight and unusual bend to his neck.

"Ki will bring Toro," Jessie said, pulling the woman after them. "Right now, we must be ready with the horses."

Minutes later they were in their saddles and watching Ki as he slipped across the dangerous open ground toward Toro. Even knowing he was there, Jessie could hardly believe the man could move so stealthily. The distance he had to travel was perhaps one hundred and twenty-five yards. Ki seemed to float across the earth and yet he blended in perfectly with the ground and occasional clumps of brush. When he reached Toro, Jessie saw the quick flash of his blade. Toro dropped into Ki's arms and writhed in pain.

Jessie took a deep breath. Bringing the semiconscious man back across that open field of ground was going to be very difficult, but if any man alive could do it, that man was Ki.

Carmen reached out and gripped her arm. "What if they see him? What then?"

"We race out there and, somehow, we try to get out of this canyon alive," Jessie answered softly, hearing the beat of her own heart grow loud in her ears.

Ki was thirty yards away when Toro suddenly roused into confused wakefulness and shouted half deliriously, "Carmen!"

His voice echoed off the canyon walls and brought the Mexicans whirling around. Because of the echoes, it took them several seconds to place the sound, and by the time that they had, Jessie and Carmen were racing forward on their horses. Ki slung the Spaniard into the saddle and then vaulted onto his own horse. Gunfire shattered the moonlit night.

"We haven't a chance that way!" Jessie shouted to Ki. "We must stampede the mustangs!"

It was their only chance, but it was a desperate one. They had discussed it and decided that if they were discovered before they could near the canyon's mouth, they would have no choice but to use a stampede as their last and only hope.

Jessie drove her spurs into her horse with Ki right beside her. She could almost feel the bullets as they penetrated and probed the night air. She whipped her frightened mount right into the rope corral and felt the animal stagger, then right itself as the ropes pulled the temporary posts loose. The corral collapsed and then Ki, Carmen, and Toro charged in to scatter the mustangs.

The revolutionaries were running toward them, shouting and emptying their guns. A mustang squealed as a stray bullet furrowed its shoulder. The squeal and the scent of blood whipped the already nervous mustang herd into a frenzy, and it was easy to scatter them toward the canyon's opening.

Jessie heard screams as revolutionaries were knocked down and then trampled by the massive herd, now possessed of only one idea—escape!

Gunfire grew ragged and she heard terrible yells. A campfire erupted in a shower of sparks as a hundred wild horses exploded through it, running mindlessly. Nothing could turn them. Men screamed, fired pistols, and waved their sombreros, but the mustangs could not be turned or stopped. A bullet scorched the air across Jessie's face. She emptied two shells and, in the semi-darkness, saw the contorted silhouette of a revolutionary twist and fall before the lead mustangs.

Jessie turned back to see Carmen and Toro riding low on the backs of their horses, while Ki was shouting and driving the herd onward. The huge tent where Armando Escobar lay in death was ripped to the earth and trampled by thousands of hooves. Now they were in the mouth of the canyon. No guards challenged them. The mustangs funneled like a great river and their current was momentarily slowed before they passed through into the next canyon.

On and on they ran until, finally, they flowed out into the desert. Like homing pigeons they circled, gathered their bearings, and wearily began to trot north toward the faraway Nevada range they once had roamed.

Dawn found Jessie, Toro, and Carmen riding wearily toward the body of Mexican soldiers up ahead. Jessie's eyes were gritty with dust and lack of sleep as she watched Mark Lyon and a brightly uniformed cadre of officers come galloping to meet them. Soldiers, some on foot and others on horses, followed in their wake. Mark and a Mexican general came galloping up to them. The officer was lean and competent-looking; his eyes missed little as he surveyed Ki, Toro, and Carmen, then returned his gaze to Jessie. "It is a great honor to meet you, Señorita Starbuck. A great honor! Forgive us for not reaching you sooner," he said with bowed head.

"It doesn't matter." Jessie pointed back to the canyon. "You will find the enemies of your government

184

back there. Armando Escobar is dead."

The general frowned. "Who killed him?"

"I did," Ki said.

"Then you have done us a great favor." The dark eyes shifted to Toro. "And who are you, Señor?"

Toro gave his name. For the moment, he was anything but handsome. His nose had been broken and his face was badly swollen from Escobar's fists. He looked nothing like the man Jessie remembered first seeing in Elko. But there was still that pride and arrogance about him, and he forced a smile to show he was not afraid. "Toro Montoya."

The general's eyes narrowed. "The famous Spanish bullfighter?"

Toro nodded. "Yes."

The general's hand moved closer to the holster at his side. "Rumor has it that you were in the United States as an agent of the revolutionaries. Is that true?"

Toro swallowed. His chin lifted and he ignored Carmen, who started to protest.

Jessie interrupted and her voice was cool and slightly indignant. "Señor Montoya is my friend and has proven himself a friend of the President of Mexico as well. He deserves to be commended for his bravery, not challenged!"

The officer blinked. Toro hid his surprise very well, but his smile widened. "Thank you, Señorita Starbuck," he breathed. "And *adiós!*"

They watched Toro and Carmen gallop unopposed south and Jessie knew in her heart that he was heading for the great bullrings of Mexico City.

"Is he really a friend of the President?" the stiff army general asked quietly.

Jessie laughed and managed to avoid the question by saying, "He proved to be so, General, and I somehow feel certain that he will become the greatest bullfighter in the history of Mexico."

The general allowed a slight smile to form at the

corners of his otherwise severe mouth. "Then you have done us all a great service."

Jessie nodded when he bowed again, and reined north on a line straight for the border. Ki and Mark flanked her stirrup to stirrup. She wondered whether the Mexican general would now order his soldiers to chase after the precious mustangs and catch as many as possible before the border, or attack the scattered remains of the revolutionary camp.

Then she remembered something—Toro had stolen a mailbag full of money from the Union Pacific Railroad baggage car, and Jessie would bet anything that he and Carmen had hidden it out here somewhere to retrieve later.

Well, I'll be damned, she thought with amusement as she swiveled around in her saddle to see their faint trail of dust lifting into the southern horizon. He got me again!